INARA
LIGHT OF UTOPIA

EDITED BY MX. YAFFA AS
INTRO EMAN ABDELHADI

MERAJ PUBLISHING

ISBN: 979-8-9894734-1-0 (Paperback)

ISBN: 979-8-9894734-2-7 (Ebook)

Cover design by Yaffa AS

Editing by Mays Salamah

Interior layout by Andrea Ramos Campos

merajpublishing.com

To the indigenous, Black, queer, disabled, and trans folks who have always seen beyond the fabric of possibility and expand it with every breath.

Full gallery of art, photos and prints that accompany these stories can be found at the QR code below:

https://www.merajpublishing.com/inara-pictures

To My Olive Tree

Mays Salamah (She/Her)

To my future olive tree, on the day of your
planting,

I may never get to taste your fruit,
Dip bread in your oil,
Or sit in your shade;
But I plant you anyway
So that the kids who call me

> Auntie

> > Khalto

> > > Aamto

Can.

And if they cannot,
Their children,

> Niblings,

> > & more

Will get to nurture you
> & enjoy all you have to offer.

meet me
  under my olive tree

we will dance
    & marvel at the moon
we will kiss
  & eat ma'amoul.

 its blossoms will fall into our curls,
       & make us laugh,
  make us think of snow
   & fill us with childlike wonder.

meet me under my olive tree
  & we will rejoice
   & be free.

Introduction

Eman Abdelhadi (She/Her)

Palestine will be free.

Palestinians will one day live dignified lives on our homeland. We will walk the streets of the old cities of al-Quds, Nablus, Nazareth and Bethlehem. We will hike the green hills overlooking Tiberius, eat oranges from Yaffa, drink the sage tea of the hills of Khalil. We will wiggle our toes in the sands of Gaza. We will wade into the sea as free people on a free land.

There will be no checkpoints, no wires, no tanks, no bombs, no missiles. Our movements will not be dictated by the color of our identification cards or the whims of concrete walls. We will roam the earth, following only the winds of fate and desire.

Palestine will be free.

Palestine is a promise. As Palestinians, we have watched the world shed our blood for 75 years; Palestine is the promise of a world that honors our humanity. We have watched the might of the dollar and the gun overrule the will of the people; Palestine is the promise of a world governed by justice not profit. We Palestinians have screamed our pain into the ether; Palestine is the promise of a world that listens.

It is our imperative and obligation to imagine that future as we fight to will it into being.
In our 2022 speculative fiction novel, *Everything for Everyone: An Oral History of the New York Commune 2052-2072* (Common Notions), my co-author M.E. O'Brien and I imagine a global revolution that transitions life out of capitalism and into a system of collective self-rule and production through communes. We imagine a world whose primary levers are not profit but care. In New York, the revolution starts with a food riot, as trans sex workers lead the fight to ensure their community is fed. But the global revolution we imagine does not begin in New

York, it begins in Palestine. Palestine liberates herself first, and the rest of the world follows.

Two years later, in the midst of a genocide in Gaza, I still believe the revolution begins in Palestine. From October 2023 to this moment (March 2024), Palestine has been liberating the world. Palestine has exposed the house of cards of Western "civilization" and "liberalism." Millions have learned our free speech is anything but free, as the hand of repression has punished anyone daring to speak up for Palestinians. We have learned that academic institutions are citadels of power not citadels of inquiry, as campus administrations have rushed to silence student support for Palestinian human rights. We have learned our votes mean little when compared with the interests of weapons manufacturers and oil companies clamoring to profit from death. Enacting boycotts of the industries participating in the oppression of our siblings in Palestine, we have had to examine the ways our lives are intertwined with that oppression. Palestine has reminded us that what we eat, what we drink, what we wear—these are all political. Palestine has exposed the intricacy of a global system that takes our money and invests it in genocide. Palestine has been liberating us.

Palestine will be free, and Palestine will free us all.

Writing Everything for Everyone during the darkness and despair of the COVID-19 pandemic was a chance to imagine a world beyond the walls currently imprisoning us. It was a transformative experience for me, because it wrestled my imagination back from capitalism. Imagining a way out of the atrocities of our current moment infused my activism with a practice of hope. I re-entered my organizing spaces energized by the possibilities of the world to come, a world we create in the microcosms of our movement work.

I have become ever more committed to hope as political praxis. Capitalism and colonialism present themselves as inevitabilities, as the natural order of things. We know that is not true. We know the world could be different, *should* be different, *will* be different. Every time we take to the streets or feed ourselves in a protest kitchen or take care of each other, we assert this truth. We are bigger than capitalism, bigger than white supremacy, bigger than settler colonialism—and we will overcome them. To commit to a political praxis of hope is to constantly ask ourselves, what will the world feel, taste, smell, look like when we win? In this anthology, queer Palestinians beckon our future, birthing freedom through prose and verse. We know the fight has not been won, but we find solace in the certainty of victory.

Grounded in Utopia

Yaffa AS (They/She)

A free Falasteen is not fiction. A free Falasteen is literally a moment away. So close we can almost taste it.

In Islam, there's a verse in the Quran that says the Divine is closer to a human being than our jugular vein. In the same way I believe that a free Falasteen is that close. It is a single blink away, potentially a single night's sleep. A single meeting, a single meal, a single hug, a single anything.

The thing is that we don't know when it will be here - it might be here by the time I'm finished writing this or the end of the time of you reading this.

As I think about the concept of utopia, a concept that in many academic spaces is seen as something created by white cis straight males - the same white straight males were also the fathers of imperialism, settler colonization and colonization - it has allowed me over the years to recognize that the world we live in is somebody's utopia, rather than thinking utopia is a far off place. For utopia is always here. The question is whose utopia?

Within *Inara*, the voices of 14 queer and trans Palestinians come together to say **our** utopia: a queer and trans indigenous utopia.

This work is a celebration of queer and trans Palestinians in all of our possibilities, moving us away from settler colonialism, colonization, imperialism, capitalism, ableism, and all the systems of oppression that we are told are indefinite. We are told that to dream of them no longer here is untenable. Yet, it is those same systems that have built this utopia for rich white cis straight males.

Utopia is not a destination and the journey is not grasping with the impossible, for utopia is always here.

Believing utopia as something unattainable is something that only benefits systems of oppression. As queer and trans Palestinians we are impacted by the world in a multitude of different ways. We are at intersects of marginalization that most people can barely comprehend. Our intersections go beyond these three identities. The vast majority of the contributors in this anthology are also disabled, many have Refugee and Immigrant experiences and when they do not, they have various levels of systemic displacement that has impacted their families for generations. We have all been impacted by settler colonialism as has every single Palestinian.

The vast majority of writers in this collection are not individuals who would normally identify as writers. For almost every single person within this anthology it is the very first time that they have explored the concept of utopia. Utopic writing is not the same as dystopian writing, as it is different parts of our brains that are engaged when we think of utopia versus dystopia. For many of us, we have never had the opportunity to develop these skill sets to engage that part of our brain, the one that is thinking about the things that we are told are impossible, and makes them a reality. As we explore utopic work we engage more and more with utopia as a practice, as a daily way of breathing, inhaling the world that exists and exhaling it out to utopia. Little by little we are able to reroute the parts of our brain so that utopian thinking becomes the norm. Utopia then becomes a probability that is closer to us than our own jugular veins.

Working through this, with the incredible writers has been such a blessing, witnessing, bringing in various modalities together, bringing essays and short stories, poetry, visual images, digital art, photography, and so much more. Throughout the collection you will notice transliteration of Arabic words and other words entirely in arabic. You will find translations to anything not easily found online in footnotes or glossaries for the different pieces. Each writer brought in their own style, their own dialect, their own being, and we want you to witness the rawness of that.

It has been such an honor working with each of the writers and artists. For me, the benefit of doing this is not having a book in the palms of my hands at the end of this process, the benefit is that the process of working together feels utopic along the way.

I would love to invite you to reflect and claim feelings of utopia as you witness and embrace this book. Allow yourself to feel utopia. Utopia is not witnessed if it is not felt. This is your invitation to feel utopia with us.

The word *Inara* in Arabic means the action of lighting a light, a light that lights other lights. It allows us to really reflect on this concept of utopia–thinking about utopia, building utopia, envisioning utopia. Feeling utopia within a community is the process of one person lighting another who lights another who lights another who lights another until we are all lit.

That light already exists within us. It is not creating something new, it is not creating light from nowhere. It is honoring that light is inherently ours. We are light. Systems of oppression will do everything they can to extinguish that light.

We are so much greater than anything they can ever be. For Humanity inherently is to be light. Humanity is to be loving and compassionate and supportive, to be intuitive, to be connected. And humanity has been here far longer than any system of oppression despite what messaging they want to send us.

Welcome to utopia!

Photos by Maria Zreiq

Photos by Maria Zreiq

Love After Return

Maria Zreiq (She/They)

I make love to you under a silent orange sky,
No warplanes, no drones, no bombs,
In a bedroom that knows freedom at last,
Under a rooftop that no one will ever take from
us

After a century of martyrdom,
After a century of birth,
I make love to you,
Upon a land, we call ours

The empire is ashes,
The sun sets untroubled,
I make love to you,
Knowing the battle is over,
And every wave in the sea,
Knows its rhythm and place

And you see me
All of me,

And I see you,

All of you;

The wounds,

The cuts,

The chaos,

The fucks,

The leftovers of exile,

The long-buried dreams,

The newly bloomed desires,

The serenity of knowing;

We returned home.

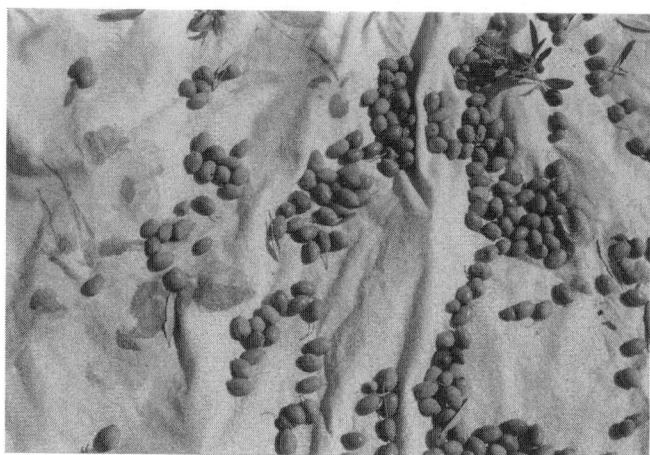

Photos by Maria Zreiq

Ancient Tears in Palestine

Maria Zreiq (She/They)

You watch the Mediterranean dancing,
I slowly peel a mandarin,
Flesh, blood, and bones,
Two mortals on the shore of the homeland.

I put a piece in your palm,
You slowly kiss my face,
I lose myself in your tenderness.

No one will ever know,
How many hearts died of longing,
for us to be here,

And no one, my love,
Can ever measure,
How much of these waves,
is made of tears.

Photos by Maria Zreiq

I Love this Part

Yaffa AS (They/She)

They smile, I smile.

Looking into the sea, feeling the red of the setting sun filling my brown skin, tingles dancing along my sides, my abdomen, my everything.

I inhale the salt in the air, filling my veins with courage and warmth. I love this part, when you see someone and for reasons beyond there's a warmth, feeling the universe parting ways for you to embrace. I love this part.

I love this part enough that I am full here and now, nothing more needed or requested.

Then they wave the next time I look over and maybe I desire a little more.

Their palm fits in mine, skin flirting and I take a deep breath.

It's the walk on the beach.

It's the staying up late around a community bonfire talking about Ghassan Kanafani, Eman Abdelhadi, Mama Ganuush, Car Nazzal, Noor Aldayeh, Duha Dahnoun, Lama, Ali Khader, Aram Ronaldo, Sonia Sulaiman, Jenan, AB Bedran, noor il alb, Maria Zreiq, رند, Mays Salamah, Haneen, Mishandi J. Sarhan all the greats of the last hundred years.

Mama Lama smiles and I wonder what she knows that the rest of us don't.

Mama Rawda tries to ask a million questions and I take their hand and run off dangerously close to the water.

Mama Kawthar is the worst though. "Did you have fun?" She asks, wiggling her eyebrows way inappropriately and I groan and run away. Not out of shame, not out of anything really but silliness. I can tell them anything, they can tell me anything, it's been like that for all sixteen years of my life.

I sleep, melting the day away and I dream of the sun setting, the sea full of blue, and love.

***

I know her from class. She knows me from Mama Kawthar.

She introduced us once, but my memory is fuzzy, so I say I know her from class, because it was in class, sitting cross legged between the olive trees that our eyes connected.

My heart felt like it didn't know how to beat anymore.

She smiled and that was that.

I love this part.

Her gaze fit in mine as she asked about Mama Kawthar.

I couldn't say a word and she smiled that brilliant smile, dimples piercing my soul as if they were made for this moment and this moment alone.

We talked about how class was going. Like me, she was an artist and wanted to explore how her art can build environmental homes. She wanted to design treehouses, allowing people to live in the heart of trees that have always been home to us. I wanted to design graves.

She raises her eyebrows at that when I say it. "For decades, humans were toxic to the land, so everytime we buried someone they actually did more harm than good to the land. We've been able to fix that with mushroom burial suits but the toxins are still in us and the land. There are some trees and plants you can grow that remove toxins from the ground. I want to design gardens that are purifying our bodies while we're still alive, as they purify the land

and the bodies we bury. They did something similar in Jenin and the Congo. Although the Congo used gemstones instead of trees. I want to do something on the cliffs here, in Yaffa."

She stops looking at me with that smile.

I'm about to say *what* when she says "I wonder if I can incorporate the same thing into the treehouses, make the walls a living and breathing extension of your work. You know in some cultures the dead are buried in the house you reside in. What would it look like if we lived in treehouses above the graves you're building, overlooking the sea, farther than the reach of the sea, transcended between the heavens and the earth."

"Let's do it," I say.

***

He doesn't know me when we meet, and it feels creepy for me to know of him, but of course I know of him.

We're at a roundtable, talking about healing the land and deepening the connection to her. He talks about the boroughs in the Congo, made of restored gemstones that were robbed from the people decades ago. How not only do these boroughs serve as altars for the 12 million who were murdered for them but they serve as a spiritual gateway, always healing, in living, in sleeping, and in death, as if we all have not heard of the structures that are now being adopted in different ways, from the selenite structures on turtle island, to the pink salt caves in the Himalayas, even to the olive tree residences in Falasteen.

"One thing that we've done to reduce flooding in the coastal cities is to build treehouse cities. Our trees are not very high or large but we found that the mix of fig and olive trees can build effective structures," I say a little later. The conversation changes from

there, moving to rituals and practices with and
for the land.

***

I remember the first time I met them. I'm three,
and we're running around a wheat field, the
place I am always home. The sun shines in their
smile, reflected in their eyes, and I'm so happy.

They were there before, of course. But this was
the moment I met them, their overgrown body,
so high up, so giant.

I didn't understand mirrors yet, but they're a
mirror. Into who I am and who I will become,
their sperm creating me, but I didn't know any
of that. I was just happy to play with the giant
in this wheat field.

Everywhere after that became the wheat field.
Their smile the first time I came home after
planting trees with the other children, mud
holding onto me like he held onto me. They

smile and I already know I'm supposed to shower outside. He takes my hand and the cold water washes over me. They dry me outside, then carry me in, sitting me in the communal kitchen.

The falafel is still hot when he puts it in front of me, with a bit of hummus, my favorite. He's my favorite.

One day I'm scribbling on a note pad, some wheatgrass and the sun setting at home. "That's beautiful," he says leaning over me without me noticing.

"Yislamo," I say.

"Can you teach me?" He asks and I nod hesitantly. I don't know why I hesitate. I've taught before, but what if... I'm not even sure, as if these thoughts are someone else's.

We do some lines together, my small hands fitting around his giant ones as I help him straighten them. His hands shake and he smiles every time. Then we do the grass, shooting up from the ground, and the sun like a smile in the distance.

We draw together every Jummah, sometimes alone, sometimes Mama Kawthar joins, sometimes Baba Munther joins, but it's always our space, they're guests.

We do this until his hands shake uncontrollably and instead I draw for the both of us, him telling me what to draw. A beach, the forest, a starry night. By then I had been taking art classes with artists from all around.

I drew him once, pretending to be drawing an elephant. He cried. I cried.

It's the first day of the week. He's lying in bed, on his side, still smiling at me. I'm twenty-six.

I draw a wheatgrass field and a sunset, the two of us staring towards it. His eyes are closed when I look up.

We bury him that evening, the picture I drew of him hanging in the common space as the community comes and holds us.

****

We're by the water, the cliffs of Yaffa behind us, the old city walls looming above. Down here we witness the waves crashing. There are four of us, we witness; waves crashing, clouds forming and breaking apart, I notice every breath. I inhale life, exhale death, and repeat the cycle.

I've been in this group ever since I could remember, but now it feels different after Baba died two weeks ago. I feel him with me, I breathe him in, and honor his release with every exhale. I feel the warmth of the tears before I'm conscious of crying.

40

"What do you need?" Maria asks from my right, barely whispering.

"To be physically held," I say and they nod, their arms wrapping around me. I cry silently with the waves.

After, I lie in the sand, allowing the smallest of particles to merge with my essence. They were once living stone, now they are living sand. I wonder what type of living and dying Baba is.

I smile as the water reaches me in that moment, rolling my eyes and then start laughing. Of course, you're the waves; both embracing and letting go in a perfect balance. I am wheatgrass, dancing in the wind, and he's always been the waves.

***

Sweat covers my eyes, I'm panting and I'm worried that I won't make it. Haifa's shores are on my right, I'm more than halfway through but I am tired. Why did I think I could do this? Everything hurts, and the endorphins they talk about seem to have fully abandoned me.

"You got this," M smiles beside me, and then I feel his arms on my shoulders, moving me forward, telling me it's okay to stop if I want to and it's okay to keep going if I want to.

I've known M my entire life. He was the first person I spoke to as a child, unable to speak to anyone else until I was 6.

"You're not the one running this marathon," I say back, still out of breath but definitely feeling better.

"I've run plenty of marathons," he says back, now running backwards ahead of me to show off.

"Fine, but where have you been? I could've used your support up in Beirut," I say.

"That was the start," he says as if he doesn't know what I'm saying.

"Yes, I needed more support at the start, I needed you to tell me not to do this to my body," I say and I know I'm not actually angry with him or myself. I'm exhausted and I'm so excited to make it to Gaza, to camp at Gaza Beach, to see Reyhan.

***

Reyhan's eyes radiate the blue of the sea, his black skin shimmering from the water. She is the love of my life.

I melt into them, as if we're not separated by space and time. They hold me and I am home.

Our tent is on the beach, the Mediterranean sprawling beyond us. Unlike the cliffs of Yaffa here it is sandy beaches for miles.

We sit on a prayer rug and stare into each other's eyes as the sun sets around me.

Her children and wife off in the distance giving us this moment, these hours, this day.

My body aches, and my soul is so full here. Always. I have loved him as he carried children, as he married, as he grew as I have, and I will watch him until my or his final breath.

***

I was named a death guide when I turned 32, when we are gifted our role in our community, a role I can change over time, but it is rare for it to be wrong. I knew it was right.

I stand above the death gardens I created in my twenties, and I walk alongside community members as they come and reflect on their own journeys.

You can not be given a role without first navigating the cycles of life and death. For without accepting and honoring both, how will you carry the sacredness of being?

Mariam smiles at me and my heart still flutters every time. I take her hand as she whispers her truths to herself. I do not say anything unless she needs me to. Most of our sessions are in silence, as she finds her way through her death.

She lost her sibling as a child, and decades later still holds onto that, no death and life group has been able to truly support her in how she needs.

"I struggle with it because why did it happen? And how could I have prevented it? Then another part of me knows that even if I had banished all water, they would still have died and I hate that about the world," she shares, speaking towards the olive trees below us.

"Then I think to myself, maybe I don't need to know the reason for it. Maybe it just is, and if it just is, then it can't be evil and I am not to blame."

She shares upwards to the fig trees surrounding us.

"Why is it so important for you to be blamed?" I ask, a question she asked me to ask when we first started, honoring that I may know when to use it.

"Because if it's my fault then it won't happen to anyone else," she says immediately and I nod, I get it.

"May I show you something downstairs?" I ask and she nods. Everyone is permitted downstairs, but not many are drawn to where bodies are washed and then buried, most are often more drawn to the rituals and ceremony out here. Our bodies belong to the land, memories belong to us.

"Have you ever seen a body washed?" I ask and she nods immediately. I don't normally ask questions I know the answers to, but this was necessary.

We enter a room filled with plants, a greenhouse of sorts, usually flooded but where plants thrive in the moisture, where bodies are washed in between.

"If your blame can be embodied in any of these plants, which would it be?"

She walks around for a bit, looking beneath surfaces and above, where there are smaller plants. At first I think she might go for one of the larger plants on the ground, instead she reaches for a small pot above with a ميموزا مستحية *mimosa pudica,* of course. I smile as she brings it towards me.

"Would you like to wash it like we wash bodies?" She nods and we move towards one of the slabs of wood in the center of the room. I hand her a small washcloth. She bows her head, muttering some prayers and I do the same.

Leaf by leaf, she lightly washes the plant. Leaf by leaf the plant withdraws, hiding in the process. Halfway through she starts laughing at the withdrawal and I laugh too.

"Would you like to bury it?" I ask Mariam and again she nods.

We walk back outside, above the treehouses to the roof gardens. She walks forward and stops at a small patch of soil, in the sun and away from the other plants. She buries it with her hands, the small shovel still in my hands, and she freezes, staring towards it all of a sudden.

I wait, and I wait, and I wait.

Then she wails, her head rising as if in a deep howl, her sound cutting through the crisp spring air. I wait, she wails, I wait, she wails, she falls backwards and I'm there to catch her. She cries then laughs and cries some more. Finally, her body relaxes, melting away as if entirely, but she holds onto her body just enough to stay.

"How did you know?" She asks a while later.

"I didn't, but you did, you've always known what you need, that everything dying deserves its moment in the sun, to be washed and buried, given back and remembered."

***

Reyhan is grey under his hijab, my black curls drift in the wind, careless for age. We're in the garden, her grandchildren in the distance exploring. I take his hand in mine and mindlessly massage it. Our wrinkles curve around one another and I lean in to kiss him as the sun disappears behind a cloud.

"I think I'm nearly there," he says as our lips part and a tear automatically falls to the side as if it had been waiting there the last six decades. I nod and squeeze her hand tighter.

It's two weeks later, two weeks of smiles and laughs, of coughs and sitting by her bedside wiping away sweat from fevers begging her to come home.

His wife and I wash his body, mapped with the life we had together, the journeys from Yaffa to Deir Al Balah.

The bonfires are so large after the burial that I can't see past them. Drums beat, children crash into water that seem still for once, dabke circles left and right.

I'm there when Hanan goes. I'm there when even the eldest goes and I see a guardian.

I head home to Yaffa for a weekend, the treehouses seem bigger than ever before. A

gust of wind blows as I open the door and I
know. I'm going home.

Art by Yaffa AS

Where Divine Love Meets You

AB Bedran (They/She)

We are singing atop the Hills of God in
Ramallah
Where my Teta attended school,
imagining her running through the treetops
with me, both of us youthful and vibrant.
Capturing her Mona Lisa smile through old
photographs in her thobe,
eternally imprinted in my DNA.
In this memory I manifest of her and me,
We are dancing among the meadows.
We are singing school songs, laughing
 making funny faces at one another through
the branches.
 We are sitting in the grass, working on tatreez.
She looks at me and tells me that this is the life
we are meant to live.
 This is enough for you and me.
Divine Love has met and always will be every
human need.

In this space we have created together, this is what is true.

I have caressed the Dead Sea.
Tasted its salt and felt the waves crash at my feet.
My best friend is there with me.
When reaching for the grapevines of Halhul,
we returned to this place where no voice is silent.
We are all affirmed by our loved ones.
Our bodies are not disregarded, our autonomy well intact.
There is no need to look for a solution,
for the promise of paradise has been delivered to us.
Since before my birth, this sense of perfection,
contentment, collective connection was not grounded in one place
but drifting throughout time as a memory.
The memory of Palestine,
realized through the expansion of healing Queer bodies.
Planting our roots down deeply,

steadfast and holy.

The rights of such sacred acts passed on
through generational blessings.

This space that exists in the far crying corners of
my father's mind.

Where he has experienced no fear for
returning,

no hatred or oppression.

No projections handed down to his first born,
me.

This body, which I love but did not ask to be
labeled, can float freely above the sea's
surface.

A Love Letter to Land

AB Bedran (They/She)

Send me
where not all of us
have known you
Within this reverie
We treat you unfallen
So gentle and kind

These spaces between nothing,
And every want or need to be met
Like strangers who become lovers
Immerse me
 in the touch of your soul
though sometimes escaping,
We are holding
All the curses and blessings,
I'll find you in our corner of the sky.

Dreamless

AB Bedran (They/She)

How many more memories to make
before days become empty?
I see that you can open me,
wondering what is to be revealed.
All we do is drink Moussy
by the secret of my mind
where a silent stream sits waiting
to hold us like a crescent.

Oh dreamless one,
reaching for stars
that burn holes in your hands,
Listen to my siren's song.
When you set sail to this territory
Did you think to crash upon my shore?

Some lucid love story come to life
from a thousand browser histories,
my legs like lips, kissing your hips,
your neck, my lips, our oneness.

Seeing the shadow of your spirit in my sleep,
now reaching for the holes in your heart.

A Moment Recurring

AB Bedran (They/She)

Like caterpillars not found in chrysalises,
Only wishing for their wings,
    Speak with your mother tongue,
    divorced from a country of origin.

No fear of loneliness can deflate us in this
climate
Painting colors on walls unseen,
illuminating forgotten stories,
    Sinking slowly in the absence of
    nation-states, how soothing.
Make way for the reincarnate,
    ancient jackal spirits, howling in the
    violet night.

Insidious aches rebirth me,
As we cling onto the bated scent
of breast milk from the crescent's bosom,
smelling of jasmine fields and wheat.

Divine Love is an Olive Tree

AB Bedran (They/She)

I saw you split the pine tree

Like God's middle finger

And you remained magnificent

For generations to behold

Divine Love is an olive tree

Hail to the branches that carry our bodies!

Legs dangling freely from greater heights

These seeds, relentlessly liberated.

Prayers to the Unknown

AB Bedran (They/She)

Inanna

    Delilah

      Ereshkigal

        Lillith

          Isis

            Hecate

              Kali

              Medusa

              Persephone

              Mary Magdalene

              The Whore of Babylon

                Fatima

              Delilah

          Lillith

        Hecate

      Medusa

Divine deities, wombed warriors

We seek refuge in your ancient wisdoms

Thresholds between the heavens and
earth
Guardians of the underworld and back
Harnessing the energy on our smallness
Rebirthing and unbirthing,
It deserves to be witnessed
Allow us to disrupt the cycles of suffering
Reclaim our agency,
May we be witnessed, wholly
The outcasts of society,
The philistines
Falasteeni.
To uplift, enlighten.
To shed our skins
Here us speak;

I AM HERE.
YOU ARE HERE.
WE ARE ALL HERE.
WE'RE STILL IN THIS TOGETHER.
WE LOVE US.
WE ARE NOT ALONE.

Pondering of Freewill

AB Bedran (They/She)

As I wait upon the lost hours,
When night is a blanket
I wrap around myself,
Holding our ancestors,
A pillar of light greets me
On the other side of the threshold.

Undoing all of me
to behold,
Glowing epiphanies

Sinking into forgotten dreams,
Soul composting
I have become the dirt
So go ahead, unearth me
Like seeds remembered, holy.

An Offering for Hind

AB Bedran (They/She)

You wake up

With the sun on your face

And you jump out of bed,

Running into the kitchen

The smell of coffee

And flowers,

Your mother's warm embrace

Your father's glowing smile

You get to play outside!

Amongst the dogs and sheep

Grazing throughout the winding path,

The hills are singing to you

You find yourself in the valley

Where a little stream meets you

You splash and play with your feet

You find rocks, turquoise and red

You run home when it gets dark

And your mother calls you for dinner

You hear stories from your father

About how the world use to be

You fall asleep in the loving arms

Of your family, they tuck you in together

This is what every day is like for you,

This is what it should be for every child.

singing the new world

noor il alb (they/them)

<u>arabic transliteration key</u>

2	=	ق / ء
3	=	ع
6	=	ط
7	=	ح

i approached the european pine.

it's time, i said, my palm touching their rough trunk. i had been able to talk to nature as a child, but trauma and displacement made me forget. i forgot so deeply that at one point, i no longer knew that this was even possible. as a young adult, i was taught how to intentionally work with plants, and with practice, i slowly remembered our ancient language once more. this communication felt like it couldn't be fully translated into words, it was a deeper exchange between our spirits, it felt like the embodiment of our oneness. now people across bilad il sham[1] were remembering how to listen to nature again so that we could steward our homelands by enacting their exact wishes.

i know, i heard the european pine say. i know i don't belong here. it feels wrong, my being here. i was never loved here, and i miss my home, even though i've never known it. i've heard the arz[2] and olive trees talking about coming back home through the mycelial network, and i want that. i want to go home, too.

i want that for you. i told the european pine. and i want you to know, we will honor your body. we will use every part of you to build our hugelkultur[3] beds to sequester your carbon.

---

[1] palestine, syria, lebanon and jordan - بِلَاد الشَّام

[2] lebanese cedar - أرز

[3]

https://www.almanac.com/sites/default/files/image_nodes/hugelkulturraisedbed.jpg
https://www.permaculturenews.org/2012/01/04/hugelkultur-composting-whole-trees-with-ease/

you will be used to create biochar, you will fertilize plants here for millennia to come. you will be part of building new life here, of restoring our indigenous ecosystem. we will plant food forests in your place that will nourish us for eons to come. the people have come to revitalize the village. but there is no place for you here.

i understand, they said.

yallah, the land whispered as a light breeze at my back encouraged me to start. i turned on my chainsaw and cut them down.

shukran, i whispered to the spirit of the fallen tree that would help us grow abundance for years to come, praying they would find their way back home.

—

i put aside the wood from the tree to prepare for the special day ahead. a descendant of a family from deir yassin had recently returned to their grandmother's house with the intention of revitalizing the village and her garden. though the 3a2edeen[4] had already had a welcome party thrown by the local musta2beleen,[5] today we were planting a food forest for them and they had invited us for a 3azoomeh.[6] we never turned down an opportunity for a celebration.

zainab and wardeh, a beautiful couple, had returned with their daughter huda and zainab's grandmother maryam. it was maryam's stone house that they had moved into. the house had been fully updated and repaired by the local trades people, with a flat stone path for maryam's wheelchair leading from the road to the house, circling the garden and future food forest which was being planted today.

---

[4] returnees - العائدين

[5] welcomers - مستقبلين

[6] feast - عزومة

70

a class from the local school came to plant the saplings around the tree stump i had just cleared. the children had lovingly grown all the saplings and gathered the seeds themselves, and would come to back to water them every week until the saplings were established enough to get their own water. after that, the food forest would be cared for by the local community. all our school children were planting trees across bilad il sham and they were well practiced now, planting and watering them as perfectly as a seasoned farmer.

one of the students, hala, began a tree planting demonstration to teach wardeh's family and other new 3a2edeen that had come with the field trip. not needing any instruction, most of the students began planting trees. hala began by teaching us how to mix soil for the different types of trees and the proper planting techniques so that we could plant our own at home.

zainab and wardeh had prepared msakhan for us all, the only thing left to do was barbeque the chicken. a few of the parents that had come with the field trip volunteered to help so that zainab and wardeh could learn to plant trees. the smoky smell of barbecued chicken and the sound of easy conversation filled the air.

then hala went over planting techniques for the various trees. when wardeh asked about what the ideal location for each type was, hala simply replied, "oh, i just ask the trees where they want to be planted." so i took my little olive sapling and we played 7amee-bared[7] until i found the right spot. as we planted them, the saplings and seeds were chattering together in delight. once my sapling was in the ground, they perked up too.

i can hear them, said my sapling, *the tree who i was cut from. they're nearby!* i smiled. as i planted an arz seed beside them, i could hear the olive sapling getting excited again.

---

[7] game of hot-cold - حامي بارد

i missed you, old friend, said the olive to the arz.

i missed you too, and i missed being here on this land. it's been so, so long, the arz seed said, relieved at finally being back in this soil.

the teacher began handing out a bowl of dates. "these are the offerings for the land spirits, so they can bless these trees and help them grow."

"thanks," i said, taking a couple of dates and placing them near the olive and arz i had planted. *shukran,* i said to the land spirits, who were now engaged in a conversation about ancestry with the new plants and the mycorrhizal fungi. they nodded in thanks, beginning to eat the dates. i turned back to their teacher. "how many trees has the class planted now?"

"this year? a thousand. and not one tree we've ever planted has died, even in the dry season," their teacher replied.

"allah ya36ekom il 3afyeh,"[8] i said.

"and now we give the trees their names," hala announced as she began handing out plaques, each engraved with the name of someone we had lost and a poem to honor their memory. after we put their plaques into the earth beside each sapling, we had a small ceremony where we each recited their name and accompanying poem as we watered. we sprinkled some wildflower and poppy seeds between the saplings and mulched around them, taking care to leave room for the seeds to sprout. then we stood back to admire our work, the tiny forest that we had planted together so quickly.

we took a break to have lunch together. the msakhan was superb, the sweetness of the

---

[8] may source grant you health - الله يعطيكم العافية

onions in a perfect marriage with the sourness of the sumac and the pungence of the cumin. zainab and wardeh had accepted the compliments gracefully, saying that it was maryam's recipe, and maryam just smiled humbly. then, we talked about the mythology surrounding the different plants. the teacher was telling the children about the folklore surrounding arz trees, and how they were related to the sumerian god ea.[9] the arz seeds were pleased to be remembered in this way, piping in to provide their version of an ancient myth, and estimated it had been at least three thousand years since their ancestors had last lived here in this village. the children's eyes grew wide at the tales, better understanding the sacredness and enormity of their work.

people in the area had heard of the family's return through the local musta2beleen, and came to drop off gifts throughout the day, as was customary for new 3a2edeen. a

---

[9] p. 259. feghali, layla k. the land in our bones: plantcestral herbalism and healing cultures from syria to the sinai. north atlantic books, 2024.

blacksmith had come to offer the use of the local metal workshop to zainab, who made jewelry. zainab's eyes sparkled with joy as they found out about all the different equipment at the shop. a couple of members of the pottery and glass collective came to drop off housewares, including a set of beautiful hand blown tiny tea glasses decorated with gold patterns. the weavers and fabric artisans dropped off warm wool clothing they had knitted and a small scarf with tatreez for maryam, decorated with the colors and patterns of this village. a local farmer came with their heirloom seeds, and wardeh surprised them with some seeds of her own which had been passed down to her from her grandparents who were lebanese and syrian. herbalists came with an herbal first aid kit, all the plant medicine and flower essences the family could need. zainab and wardeh had tried to pay the artisans for their gifts but everyone refused. they had made a huge amount of food, and everyone who came was invited to come eat or take some food home.

"how are you doing?" i asked zainab, noticing the slightly overwhelmed look in their eyes.

"i'm good..." they said, trailing off as they stared at everything they had received. "this is just a lot of gifts. and from people i don't even know."

"yet," i said, "people you don't know yet." i smiled, remembering how i had to adjust to the generosity of our people when i first arrived, unused to receiving as much i gave. "it was an adjustment for me too, when i first came back. i'm still working on receiving and reciprocity. welcome home." zainab smiled.

i spotted ameena arriving, saying "il 7amdoullah 3al salameh"[10] to the 3a2edeen and greeting each and every person. her pace was slow and leisurely, and she walked with the ease and grace of people who have been blessed by inana herself.

---

[10] thank source for your safe return - الحمد لله عالسلامة

"mar7aba!" ameena said, as she sat on the bench beside me. she was part of the council that oversaw the stewardship of our natural resources. while each of our communities was self-governing, councils were created to coordinate the distribution of resources across bilad il sham so that we could support each other. ameena was also a flower essence practitioner. "i like connecting people to what they need," she had told me when i first met her, "whether it be resources or the right flower essence."

"perfect timing! i saved you a plate," i told ameena.

"shukran!" she said, beginning to eat.

"how was your day?"

"i slept for longer than usual, which is good cause i had an amazing dream. and on my way here i met a flower who wanted to be made into an essence."

"ooo which one?" i asked

"zahret il barakeh.[11] do you want to try some?"

"that's one of my favorites, yes, thank you" i said as i got out my water bottle for her to place a few drops into.

"i'm going to make a post on the natural resources forum to let people know the wood is available here," i told her. "do you know if anyone's looking for any?"

"the community garden at deir il bala7 need some wood to make biochar and hugelkultur beds," ameena said between mouthfuls. "they're planting a food forest underneath the date palms. they also need sawdust for their humanure system.[12] and the residents of nabi saleh are building a garden around their spring."

---

[11] flower of blessings (nigella flower) - زهرة البركة

[12] see http://humanurehandbook.com/downloads/Huma nure_Manual_2019.pdf

"oh, i'm actually going to gaza city later, i can take the wood to deir il bala7 to save them the trip."

"perfect," said ameena, making appreciative noises as she took another bite of msakhan.

i picked up my phone to make the post, the same one i had had for a long time now. after the congolese people had reclaimed their natural resources, they closed down all their mines. their scientists had estimated that if the minerals that had already been mined were reused indefinitely, no new minerals would ever need to be mined again. they created new global standards concerning the use of technology, and now every device using their minerals would last decades in order to honor the earth's resources. as they collected reparations, the congolese people also began a process of repair, where all of us who were complicit in their harm showed up for their healing in the ways they asked us to, one of

many such collective processes of repair
happening on the planet.

after finishing our food and cleaning up, we all
sat in a circle in the new food forest and did
some healing work together. i taught the
children how to channel healing energies, and
they took turns healing first themselves and
then each other. we talked about how we
need to get the other person's permission
before sending them energy, and how it was
completely up to us if we wanted to accept
the energies offered to us or not. little bubbles
of different colored energies filled the air as the
children took turns gifting and receiving
healing energies. one kid, hilal, kept laughing,
insisting that the soft pink energies 3ali had sent
them tickled. after that, everyone was in
laughing fits from either the pink energies or
the contagious laughter that ensued.

"more?" huda managed between laughs.

"yes!" hala answered, laying on the earth,
shaking from laughter. "wait, no, no more." she

waved away the pink bubble to keep it outside her aura. she stood, trying to regain her breath. "do *you* want some?" she asked a fig sapling.

yes, they said. hala offered the bubble to the fig tree, and then we all got to find out what it sounded like when a fig tree laughed, radiating joy and their small branches shaking lightly in the wind.

i showed the children how to make energetic containers to protect the plants, around each tree and the forest as a whole. we made sure each of the seeds and saplings were grounded in their new home and accessing all the energies they needed. i led us in a healing to help the new plants grow and adapt to their new home, to heal the land spirits and the land so that this new ecosystem would thrive.

"may this forest bring us abundance for generations to come. may the spirits of our loved ones be watered and nourished by the trees planted in their memory," said the teacher.

"ameen," we all replied. we had a moment of prayer as we began imagining the forest to come: the trees growing tall, the spirits of our loved ones being healed, the families that would pick olives here together. i imagined the village growing strong, zainab's family feeling rooted in love and belonging as they grew old here. i could smell the perfume of the fig trees, tall and ripe with fruit, their lush green leaves extending like hands to embrace the sun. we envisioned our people harvesting pine nuts, apricots, grapes, dates, and figs, being so abundantly blessed that they could share with other communities. we imagined families sitting together under the shade of the trees, surrounded by the enchanting scent of damascus roses, sharing birthday sweets year after year. i could see a father and his young daughter playing hide and seek among the now wide tree trunks, with her giggling giving her away every time.

"za2a6tek!" her dad said as he rounded a fig tree, picking his daughter up in his arms and lifting her up in the air, her screams and giggles of pure joy echoing across time.

—

i waved to the shepherd and his sheep, waiting until they crossed the road before starting my solar powered truck. my car was powered by a new design invented by a young student at birzeit university. it was so highly efficient that the car could run even on cloudy days or at night on stored solar power alone. this open source design was now widely used across bilad il sham due to the ease of using it to convert obsolete, fossil fuel based cars into solar powered ones. it was so effective that solar power became our main form of energy, and the new solar panels lined our roofs and powered our devices.

i began driving, the verdant countryside my constant companion. i passed lush, green hills full of saplings and dotted with wildflowers.

small villages nestled into the hillsides, looking as if they had sprouted from the earth. i went to drop off some wood and sawdust to a community garden in deir il bala7, and stopped by gaza city on my way back.

i looked around me, amazed by how gaza city had been truly transformed. all around me, the clean, wide streets were lined with rebuilt and restored buildings made of low carbon, self healing concrete that towered over me, interspersed with shorter straw bale cob houses. i could hear the sound of children playing, people laughing. i could smell bread and mana2eesh. in the distance, i heard various bird calls from the newly restored wetlands. the only things i could see in the sky was an eagle flying in slow, wide circles and the bright, beaming sun warming my skin and heart. people were all around me, finally free to live their lives on their land.

i met a few of my loved ones at a beach near gaza city. first, we placed offerings of rose and hawthorn on the altar created for all those we had lost. we made sure that their memories lived on. their loved ones wrote stories and created art honoring them so their truth would never die. roads, schools, buildings carried their names. we planted trees in their memory, and named gardens, olive groves and forests after them to immortalize them in their homelands; they became part of the land itself. we tended altars and prayed for them, so that the spirits of those whose deaths still tethered them to this earthly plane would heal and ascend, would rejoin our well ancestors and source, so they would be free. we communicated with all those we had lost through the veil that separated our worlds, so they were still here with us even in death, for nothing could destroy their spirit, their divine spark, and nothing could keep them from their homelands ever again.

we gave gratitude to all those who had guarded, nourished and affirmed life. their countless acts of courage and bravery invited us to step into more of ourselves, more of our true power everyday. their selfless sacrifices transformed their spirits into angels, into well ancestors, into guardians of our homelands. it was deeply humbling to be in the presence of beings who held such integrity in their hearts, whether they still lived amongst us or had passed on.

—

a few years ago, just before Indigenous nations across turtle island reclaimed their reparations and lands back, when i had been living as a settler on the territories of the q̓íc̓əy̓, q̓ʷa:n̓ƛ̓ən̓, and kʷikʷəƛ̓əm nations, blue vervain was teaching me about the importance of wetlands. i learned of a project that restored a wetland on nearby xʷməθkʷəy̓əm, Sḵwx̱wú7mesh, and səl̓ilw̓ətaʔɬ territories, where it only took two years before the salmon returned to spawn in their ancestral birthplace after not being able to return. i felt in awe of the resilience of life, and how quickly things could come into balance if humans created the conditions for life to thrive. i had wondered, how many generations of salmon had kept the knowledge of their ancestors' birthplace hidden safe in their hearts even though they themselves had never been born there? how did they keep hope alive, still seeking to return every spawning season regardless of how much time had passed? how did they feel when they finally returned?

those salmon gave me hope in my heart that return would be possible for all beings, that i too could return to my homelands. so in the time before my return, i fueled the sumud in my heart with nature's resilience, the seemingly small miracles that were all around me if i stopped to listen: the hummingbirds, the return of salmon to a wetland after generations, a cedar tree that had almost been uprooted but with the help of its neighbors survived to grow as tall as any other tree in the forest.

i didn't always know it but i had always been returning home in so many ways: to my ancestors, to my homelands, to myself. like a salmon, i too kept my ancestral birthplaces hidden deep in my heart, and was guided to return by an inner compass, an ancestral momentum, an impulse so deep it was partly unconscious. before i could physically return, it was my ancestral plants that opened portals to allow me to return energetically.[13] and then the land began calling me home.

—

after paying our respects, we went swimming. impossibly, it was still afternoon. there was an expansiveness to time here, where each day stretched out to an eternity like they did when i was a child, every hour as long as our shadows when the sun was low in the sky. there was always more than enough time for everything.

i took a deep breath, savoring the smell of the saltwater sea. its waves were softly lapping at the shore, too many shades of blue to describe, the light of the sun dancing atop its rippling waters in mesmerizing sparkles. the

---

[13] p. 43. feghali, layla k. the land in our bones: plantcestral herbalism and healing cultures from syria to the sinai. north atlantic books, 2024.

warm, clear seawater was perfect for swimming, and i spent as much time as i could feeling the love of the sun and sea on my skin.

fa2dtek ya 7abeebty,[14] i told the sea as i waded in, sprinkling rose petals on the waves as an offering, every muscle in my body automatically relaxing as i began floating on my back. the sea answered not with words but a surge of love, rocking me gently with its waves.

before coming back, i didn't know, couldn't imagine what it felt like to belong to a land. but here i was, feeling so rooted on these lands, so embodied that i could feel every cell in my body vibrating. floating in the gentle expanse of a sea that intimately knew and loved me, i felt so happy and free in my heart. i was enveloped by the divine love that i once thought had forsaken me but that had always been there, patiently waiting for me to let it into my heart again. a sense of wholeness permeated my body and soul, a wholeness

---

[14] i've missed you my beloved - فقدتك يا حبيبتي

beyond what i thought i would ever be able to experience in this lifetime. held by my ancestral waters, greeted by every tree, surrounded by the plants that had shaped the dna of my entire lineage,[15] i felt like a part of the land itself. emerging from the sea, my soul and body felt cleansed, my heart open.

shukran ya 7abeebty,[16] i thanked the sea.

3afwan ya 7ubby,[17] the sea said.

the beach was filled with people. the atmosphere was warm and celebratory togetherness. now that people had everything they needed, we could take our time to enjoy life and be with each other. nearby, where the beach met a community garden, a jasmine was thriving among the trees, its sweet, floral perfume transporting me back to my

---

[15] p. 43. feghali, layla k. the land in our bones: plantcestral herbalism and healing cultures from syria to the sinai. north atlantic books, 2024.

[16] thank you my beloved - شكراً يا حبيبتي

[17] you're welcome my love - عفوًا يا حبي

childhood. underneath it, a group of elders were playing tableh and singing a folk song to a nearby olive tree.[18] the olive tree was thoroughly enjoying being honored through song, its branches waving happily in the wind. as they sang, i noticed neighbors and passersby occasionally stopped to join in. once, a person who happened to be carrying a oud even joined them for a song, her prosthetic fingers playing the strings without missing a note. their eyes widened in surprise but they didn't stop, the beach slightly quieter as people started listening in. that song earned the whole group applause and zaghareet.[19]

farther away to my right, there was a group of young people dancing dabke to music blasting from a portable speaker, improvising their own moves mixed with the traditional ones. they were surrounded by a group of onlookers who were clapping along to the music and adding "he2! he2! he2! he2!" on the up beat. on the other side, two men were

---

[18] https://bit.ly/3TOzY3N

[19] ululations - زغاريت

celebrating their wedding, a grandma gifting them with a mawal.[20] their party clapped for them as they shyly adorned each other by placing wreaths of flowers on each other's heads.

people had brought incredible picnics or were barbecuing their dinner on the beach, which meant that the smell of delicious foods was everpresent. following the smell of cinnamon and allspice to its source, we had found ma2loubeh made by a smiling tata[21] and sido[22] with the help of their extended family. they wanted to gift us some ma2loubeh and we gifted them some of the idreh khaliliyeh my friends had made. it turned out that sido was originally from il khalil where idreh comes from. he closed his eyes after trying a bite of the rice, chickpeas and goat meat, before giving us the highest of praises: "zey idret immy."[23] i also

---

[20] a type of singing traditionally performed at weddings to bless the married couple - مَوّال

[21] grandmother - تاتا

[22] grandfather - سيدو

[23] like my mother's idreh - زي قدرة إمي

insisted that the community garden at deir il bala7 had given me too many apricots for my friends and i to be able to finish so they accepted a small basket of the fruit as well.

the smoke from argileh lit with fa7em sindyan[24] wafted by, fruity and light. there was a young person celebrating their birthday, elated by the gifts, sweets and love they were being showered with. their friends and family sang sana 7ilwa[25] to them and fed everyone who happened to be nearby with their homemade knafeh to celebrate. i went back to pay my compliments to the chef, their middle aged father with a round belly and deep creases around his eyes from always laughing. i gave him some apricots as we exchanged jokes and recipes over meramiyeh[26] tea.

---

[24] lebanese oak coals - فحم سنديان

[25] happy birthday - سنة حلوة

[26] a type of sage - مريمية. latin name for this variety is salvia fruticosa according to p. 231. feghali, layla k. the land in our bones: plantcestral herbalism and healing cultures from syria to the sinai. north atlantic books, 2024.

instead of clashing with each other, the different noises somehow blended together easily to form a festive atmosphere, and it filled me with happiness to hear the sounds of joy and laughter along with the soft whooshing of the ceaseless ocean waves. as i looked around me, i saw how even lighter skinned people like me had darkened after spending so much time worshiping the sun and loving our land. surrounded by a sea of palestinians, brown and Black, all of us so happy and carefree, i felt the joy of returning home anew. no matter how much time had passed, the joy of my 3awda[27] continued to gush like an eternal spring, like a beautiful surprise: when i was surrounded by people who mirrored the generosity and kindness of my own heart, in the soft scent of the upright, purple irises, in the way the sea held my heart, in the sun's rays breaking through the clouds after a rain, in the deep embrace of belonging i felt while being celebrated by my soul family, my well ancestors, and my homelands.

---

[27] return - عودة

the sunset was a wonder, with the orange horizon transforming into stunning hues. the clouds reflected the pink light on their underside, fading to purple. the sea reflected everything, doubling its beauty. people all around me were trying to photograph it, but i knew its breathtaking beauty could never be truly captured. a group of people traveled farther away to my left to make wudu and perform evening prayers together.

then my loved ones and i began our own ritual. we purified our energy in the ocean. letting go of what was not truly ours and asking for all parts of us to return home to our bodies. we stood outside a cave by the beach farther away from the crowds, the location of which we had divined from piecing together the clues from our dreams.

it was night now, the stars brighter than usual in the presence of the dark moon. inside the cave, the bioluminescence cast a beautiful light blue glow over everything. the cave thrummed with energy and ancient magic, the waves inside echoing infinitely. we had practiced this prayer before, in many places. each place held a different power, a different type of magic that the colonizers had previously tried to extract. but our ancestors and the land spirits had guarded them too well, the places hidden and their guardians powerful and well fortified. there were safeguards in place to stop the magic from flowing into the land, to keep the wellsprings of magic from falling into the wrong hands, and now we were restoring the flow of magic to bring healing to the land and all its beings.

"do you have it?" my friend asked.

"yes, yes, of course." i rummaged in my backpack and removed a jar. it had sa7lab made with rosewater and honey, something the cave and its guardians had specifically requested. we made an altar with the offering, greeting the land and its beings, introducing ourselves and offering gratitude and prayers from our hearts.

"may we have permission to do our prayer in this cave?" i asked.

yes, i heard a voice from within, coming from the land itself. the other nodded to me: they had heard it too. we entered deeper into the cave, putting down cushions so people could sit if they needed to. we formed a circle, the warm waves still reaching between my feet.

i began singing, a few low notes before transitioning to high ones. my loved ones echoed me. in creation, everything has a vibration, and sound can call in form, so we were singing the new world into existence, together. when we finished, we were left only with the sound of the echoing waves. then, a multicolored flickering light appeared in mid-air before us, growing, expanding into a sphere. my heart swelled, i exchanged looks of awe and gratitude with my circle: we had opened the portal.

the sparkling rainbow magic from the wellspring began spreading through the cave

and beyond, bringing healing to bilad il sham
and all its beings. as i began singing again, i
saw the pain of my ancestors being
transmuted. i felt their power flowing through
me, mixing with the magic of the land that was
returning to my body. my ancestors' hard work,
their love and sacrifice, their resilience and
courage had already created a new world for
me, giving me opportunities to fulfill my path,
bringing me back to my homelands. i was
determined to keep creating a better future
for all those who would come after me. when i
sang, the trauma of displacement that had
uprooted my whole lineage, that had harmed
us and caused us to create harm, that had
persisted generation after generation, that
trauma began to be held by the earth and
universe, began to be healed and transmuted
into pure power, pure creative energy.

we began dancing, the ancestral rhythms in
our dna guiding us, our bodies flowing like
water. as we sang, our well ancestors
surrounded us, singing a separate but
complementary part. then our descendants

arrived, completing the circle, singing their own harmony that blended seamlessly with ours. we formed a circle, unbroken and whole. we were dancing together, past, present and future converging into one. the healing frequencies from our song reverberated across all of time and creation. we were so wholly anchored here, in our bodies, on this land, with these plants, on this earth. in our hearts was the prayer for a better future, for freedom, wholeness, healing. that profound love was transformed into song at our throats. plant and animal spirits appeared beside us to join in. the arz, olive trees, roses and flowers swaying to the music. a regal lioness watching us silently with love in her eyes, her cubs playing at her feet. otters were diving into the sea in one fluid motion. the land spirits made themselves seen, adding their own melody full of otherworldly beauty. there was a vibration like a heartbeat coming from the land under our feet, echoed by the waves: the earth and ocean had joined our call. our prayers for miracles and divine intervention were heard by the angels, by source themself. they knew we were ready now. we could not be held down any longer:

chains were breaking, curses were dissolving,
veils were lifting, contracts were ending.

with our song, we began praying that future
generations on this earth would be so free that
they could not even begin to comprehend
what we had gone through. we prayed that all
humans would learn freedom, repair and right
relationship, true justice and peace. we began
dreaming that humanity on this earth would
explore joy, love, pleasure, beauty,
abundance. we prayed that we would repair
our relationship with this planet and all its
beings. as the portal in the center of our circle
was opening, we could see, feel, hear and
smell this future as if it were here already, as if
we were there already. to me, this new future
felt like rosewater on my heart, a sigh of relief,
a gentle expansion, like being able to fly. it
smelled of damascus roses, fresh honey and
arz needles. it felt like the tranquility of a sacred
forest and the sweet joy of a celebration all at
once. and so much more that was impossible
to put into words. to experience our future
homelands and all their beings so whole and

free was itself a healing, and we made this feeling available to our people so we could collectively dream this future into existence together.

i began sending a telepathic message to guide my past self to this moment, *"our people survive the genocide. empire has crumbled. palestine is free. we have liberated bilad il sham.* i have returned to our homelands like so many others. we are healing and thriving on our land. we are birthing the new earth. you know in your heart that we can get free, even if you can't always feel it. i need you to keep going. remember the impossible miracles that have already gotten you this far. keep dreaming of a better future. keep singing it into existence. i know you can't see it now but out of this unfathomable loss and grief is a path towards healing, towards a future that is better than you could ever imagine. *sammed,*[28] keep hope alive in your heart. keep praying for miracles. see beyond the confines of your current reality and feel me now, here, alive,

---

[28] stay faithfully steadfast - صمّد

heart beating, calling you forward to the near future. i live, i survive, i thrive but only if you choose to keep going. be brave. i love you."

Art by Mishandi J Sarhan

My Homeland

Sonia Sulaiman (She/Her)

She is the streets of Ramallah after nightfall,
quiet and peaceful,
with short bursts of energy and sound.
I love the streets of Ramallah after nightfall.

She is the courtyard of Al-Aqsa,
tranquil and safe,
the feeling of home at first glance.
I love the courtyard of Al-Aqsa.

She is the rocks on the shores of Akka,
solid enough to lean on,
warm to the touch, fitting perfectly in my
hands.
I love the rocks on the shores of Akka.

She is a fresh orange in Yaffa,
bright and tangy and sweet,
melting beautifully on my tongue.
I love the fresh oranges in Yaffa.

She is the markets in Nablus,
rich with culture,
the faint aroma of knafeh lingering near.
I love the markets in Nablus.

She is my homeland,
always leaving me with a sense of longing,
and an underlying tone of belonging.
I love my homeland.

In my homeland,
she and I are both free.
We wander the streets of Palestine,
and I show her what she is to me.

I feed her the oranges that are just like her
tone,
and let my fingers linger on her smooth and
warm lips,
before showing her the rocks that fit like she
does.

I walk her through the markets that smell like
her breath,

and the courtyard that feels like being in her
embrace,

and listen to her laugh on the streets of my
hometown.

She is my homeland,

She makes me feel free.

She pulls me away from dim reality.

I love my homeland.

She

Sonia Sulaiman (She/Her)

They call Palestine "She"

She's beautiful, sights that make you crave more.

She smells good, the air lingers with blossoms.

She's aging gracefully, scarred from battle.

They call Palestine "She"

She's beautiful, enjoying the sights with me.

She smells good, like blossoms and summer.

She's aging gracefully, her scars delicate to my touch.

There is She and there is Palestine.

Both their touches are welcome, longed for.

They make me feel alive, the best version of me.

I love her because she is my Palestine.

Art by Yaffa AS

To a Day When the Colors Change

Sonia Sulaiman (She/Her)

To a day when Red symbolizes poppies.

To a day when Black is simply the night sky.

To a day when White is the chirping peace doves.

To a day when Green olive trees are free to grow and live for generations to love.

To a day when the colors change.

Beneath the Olive Branches

Sonia Sulaiman (She/Her)

"This floor is so rocky, can't we sit somewhere else?"

I roll my eyes at the silly request.

Where else in this grove of trees on mountain tops do you plan to rest?

Beneath the hot sun, my skin grows tanner by the minute.

A warm, golden shade.

How wonderful it is to wander these groves,

Bathed by the sun's rays.

Beneath the open sky, the air occupies my lungs.

A satisfying feeling.

The air is magically allergen-free,

My homeland is so healing.

Beneath the olive branches with their
generational tales,

You lay still by my side.

I count to you the fruits on branches,

My eyes open wide.

Beneath my watchful irises you suddenly rise,

Your interest is piqued.

You stand in my shoes

And absorb my home's mystique.

Art by Summar

Palestinian Care Manifesto

By Jenan (She/Her/Any)

"جانا عونة يا إبراهيم ريح اليوم يا ابراهيم فيها النصر يا إبراهيم"

-Palestinian Folk Song

Ma'dud is a bamboo-like stick used for gauging the level of water in a reservoir. The stick is measured with tape and equally divided into sections according to the number of cultivating families in a clan. The sections are marked with thorns stuck into the stick. The stick is placed inside the reservoir, and the collection of water starts from sunrise until sunset. The division of water supply is repeated among different clans who own mashakeb (nearby cultivated plots of land). The water moves from the reservoir to the respective lands through qanawat (canals). Irrigators respect each other's rounds, determined by the time allocated that corresponds to the Ma'dud that they own. Each cultivator is responsible for being present to collect their water amount. If a cultivator forgets to show up, someone from their family will collect the water for them. When one cultivator finishes watering their land, the next cultivator at the pool shuts the water flow for them. The system repeats every four to eight days, depending on the type of crops. If less water is needed than the allocated Ma'dud, a family can decide to give the excess water to a clan in need. Ma'dud is an ancient Palestinian management system. Ma'dud is a bamboo stick. Ma'dud is a water share, and more broadly, a resourceful share. Ma'dud is a livelihood.

Art by Jenan

Care is a bamboo stick; care is resurgence. When we practice care in a Free Palestine, we are reclaiming socio-cultural modes and traditions connected to the land, to nature, and to each other, that were lost or suppressed. A Free Palestine involves openness–openness to reimagining Palestinian sovereignty as an embodied claim to the land. Care in a Free Palestine shies away from the idea that neoliberal markets can deliver mechanisms of care.

Concepts of interdependence are crucial to how Palestinians operate in the world. This sense of interdependence is present in management systems such as Ma'dud, that aim to bring the various pieces of our lives together. The cartography of Ma'dud can be mapped onto other intimate social processes; specifically, we use it as a guideline that shows how care is organized and displayed. Ma'dud allows us to think of limitless pathways for care. We practice care that makes safe spaces for everyone, and harnesses realism to support each individual's needs.

If a community member is in need of more resources, other community members share their resources for the sake of maintaining harmony.

Care is a communal system that is not monopolized by a single person or institution. Care takes into consideration that if something in the system breaks down, everybody is informed.

Care is based on solidarity and accountability, and is constantly re-configured as a cultural space according to the complex relationships between people.

Care is a mode of being; Ma'dud is a mode of care. Care is collective, and collective care becomes collective action.

Care embodies answers of how we live, and how we live together. Care invokes practices and values that are foundational to Palestinian knowledge.

The core Palestinian values that inform how we practice care are Ouneh (collaborative support), Faz'a (impromptu help), Sharaka (cooperation), Tabadul (reciprocity), O'sareyyeh (familiality), Karam (generosity), and Hikaye (story-telling). These values require us to respond to social, cultural, ancestral, terrestrial, spiritual, and temporal species activities that make up inter-related life processes.

Ouneh is a concept deeper than volunteering. Ouneh is an informal social institution that emerged with the goal of filling shortages in community work. It is present in the way Palestinians help each other build houses, and join to assist each other in the olive harvest season. The host families provide food and ensure the participants' needs are met.

Another value related to Ouneh is Faz'a. Faz'a takes on a spontaneous and emergency-like collective action in order to help a person or people in need. Faz'a requires vigilance towards others' crises, and takes on the form of a human chain; where every member of our community strengthens others, and nourishes our ties together.

This is where O'sareyyeh would come in, where the concept of familiality between Palestinians is not limited to clans or blood ties; O'sareyyeh is based on a consensual logic of shared identity, politics, histories and experiences grounded in mutual respect that allows Palestinians to move along with each other with ease and familiarity. Palestinian O'sareyyeh becomes an extension of Palestinian land, where a return to the land is also a return to each other.

Care for us hinges on Tabadul. Tabadul is a form of reciprocity that involves a mutual giving and receiving based on good relations. Tabadul is not constructed around a linear time frame; in an agricultural system, a cultivator may give another cultivator seeds for one year, and the other cultivator may share seeds in the next year. Tabadul ensures the wellbeing of its participants: there is no accounting in Tabadul, and if a participant fails to give back, they are not cut off- instead, they are encouraged to give back in other ways. This principle leads to a praxis of care that is not merely charitable or altruistic.

118

Rather, it is mutually beneficial and harmonious, and it centers internal consistency.

Another associated value is Sharaka, which is co-operation. Sharaka as a system emerged from sharecropping, where a piece of land can have various permutations that belong to different people. Sharaka informs our way of care by forming relationships that connect us cooperatively, allowing us to share resources, and express our limitations.

Karam is interwoven with all other values, and as a concept, it signifies generosity and hospitality, and rids of an expectation of compensation. Karam comes from a belief in Palestinian culture that all natural resources are a ne'mah (gift) from God, and cannot be individually owned. In fact, it is very common in Palestine for people to pick fruit from a neighbor's tree, without fear of reprimand. Karam is incorporated into our matrix of care by treating other community members with nobility and honor. Karam increases affection and symbiosis in a caring network and trains our souls to be abundant.

Care, for us, has a practical responsibility of bridging a clear understanding in the relationship between the past, present, and the future. One way of creating this bridge is by disseminating knowledge and wisdom through Hikaye. Hikaye is an oral method of storytelling that focuses on real or imagined tales most commonly practiced by Palestinian women to provide localized perspective and societal critique. Through Hikaye, we create a space for a cross-generational sharing of stories, narratives, and experiences that inspire a pedagogical wonder. Hikaye comes to take on the role of an interactive participation in care. The information and stories shared mediate dialogue between community members and enrich encounters by adding meaning, value, and resonance to the care work being undertaken.

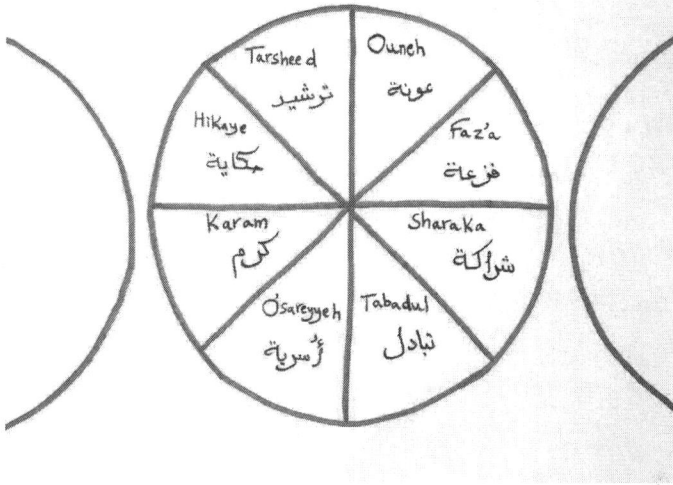

Art by Jenan

Care is an act of world-making and belonging. Even though our matrix of care is transformative, we recognize that native voices are not homogenous, and what works for some may not work for others. Our politics of care is oriented towards relations rather than identities, because in Palestinian spaces, there are multiple identities that do not sing in unison.

Care networks are built out through time, and take into account different lived experience, and how differently people encounter such spaces; care spaces are constantly evolving. Care for us is also about the advent of something new, and the opening of *cosmophonies*- in other words, care makes new worlds manifest or appear.

Our praxis of care invokes the value of abundance, or opening up to the rest of the world, which demonstrates the need to translate the potential of care into proximal communities. This is the final principle of Tarsheed: rationing care resources and sharing. This principle consolidates the notion that the Palestinian body is inherent in the land of Palestine, and the land of Palestine is inherent in the world; accordingly, the Palestinian body is inherent in the world. From here arises collective interdependence and a responsibility to sustain the world.

Care is a way of belonging that ruptures space and time. If our current of care instigates belonging, then belonging is a movement that involves reciprocity and participation, where it is constituted by those who belong to it in such a way that also belongs to them. Palestinian belonging unfolds a type of space that corresponds to us, or opens up a space within our place in the world.

Care permeates belonging and allows
Palestinians to inhabit the world in our own
way, thus bringing it together. By opening up
to the world each in their own way,
Palestinians are in a collective relationship with
more of the world, we are present in the world
and also the world is present in us to the same
reciprocal extent. Belonging grounds
participation in the world, and the world gives
unity to our being. Through this work, the
unveiling of our mechanisms of care ground us
as harmonious beings with all of our
surroundings.

Shukr:

My essay is inspired by intellectual rumination
on several authors' previous scholarship. I am
much indebted to the work of Janan Mousa in
her 2020 paper, "Collective Action in an
Exceptional Governance Context: A Critical
Analysis of Co-operative Water Management
in the West Bank of Palestine", Renaud
Barbaras's (2019) "Belonging: towards a
phenomenology of the flesh", Olivier

Vallerand's (2013) "Home is the Place We All Share", Hamdan Taha and Iman Saca's (2022) "Invoking Awneh: Community Heritage in Palestine", Marian Barnes et. al (2015) *Ethics of Care: Critical Advances in International Perspective*, and Jamal Nabulsi's (2014) "'to stop the earthquake': Palestine and the Settler Colonial Logic of Fragmentation", as well as his 2023 article, "Reclaiming Palestinian Indigenous Sovereignty", and Stephanie Butler's 2020 review, "Indigenous Resurgence". I am also indebted to the land- our Palestinian land- with all its stones, its skies, its plants, animals, elders and children, from which several ecological experiences have emerged to endow me with practical and theoretical knowledge. Finally, I am indebted to our Palestinian peers on the ground, the purveyors of carework, who spend time caring for our country, in order to embrace us all in a Free Palestine.

First Kiss

Yaffa AS (They/She)

his name sits

on my lips

where it belongs

swirling on the insides

of my gums.

I didn't know

names could

live inside our

being until the

first kiss in

Falasteen

Art by Mishandi J. Sarhan

When I die

Yaffa AS (They/She)

my body will be
cleansed in Jenin
above every
ancestor

there'll be a
procession from
Jenin to Al-Aqsa
where they will
pray side by side,
a rainbow of being
bowing to Allah
behind, above,
encircling
my body

they will carry
me to Yaffa and
bury me in a citrus
grove, where olive,

fig, and pomegranate
trees stand guard
as Yaffa Oranges
reclaim my body

but I will
not be present
for I will be home,
back, one with
Allah
careless of the
utopia I leave
behind

Art by Yaffa AS

Musings of a Teenager

Yaffa AS (They/She)

I wonder if she
likes me
does she know?
I'm tangled in her curls
the humidity frizz
locking me in

Mama says to
ask her out.
she doesn't get it
what if she does?
am I ready?
two months from
my naming ceremony

they fill
my thoughts
during olive harvest
beach days
as I sketch Yaffa's

walls again and again
as if there's some
hidden wisdom there

she smiled at me
one morning
my breath catches and
I can't breathe
does anyone else
ever feel this way?
Baba says yes
most people do on the
romantic spectrum
I tell him he must
be wrong
how could anyone
function if so?
he laughs, then Mama and Ren
and I groan
cramps filling my
heart

I know everything

about her,
best friends from
before the beginning.
Ren says all our souls
recognize each other
from lives we may never
remember, lived fully.
I wonder if we've lived
this before

I ask one day,
under the shade of
the fig trees overlooking
the world,
they smile and take
my hand,
it's everything then
until their lips are
on mine and
I wonder if maybe
breathing from lungs
is temporary
until lips are filled

with oxygen
if I never breathe again
I'll live forever
then her hands glide
on mine and I'm a
Supernova
cheesily combusting
into a black hole??

then, more
then, they're there
for dinner
like she normally
is and I can't stop
smiling
ear to ear
wondering, is my entire
being a smile?

I draw her sometimes
in the fields,
in classes we share,
from my mind

over years and lifetimes
our first dance
the second the
third, the everyday
before, during, and after

we hold hands
smile, cry, as if stuck
in every emotion
holding onto the
one beyond them
love

there are kisses
hands held with other
smiles, my skin on
theirs, nourishing one
another

I draw a sea
of love, bodies
in ecstacy connecting
beyond time and space

I am there

she is there

talking about

bits and pieces of

life that make

us whole

home becomes

shared space between

us and others

I draw them all

they farm, their fruit

filling our bellies

they fill the gaps

between us

Our eggs coalesce

materializing in a child

that is neither of ours

yet part of everything

we are

she claims

Avé, they say
Adam and Eve were
one first,
a cycle of loss
and growth
complete

we explore wheat fields and
mentorship structures,
we find their soul
belongs in the sea
I follow them in,
the water too cold
for my lungs

I draw them too,
a speck so physically small
in a passionate sea,
yet larger than passions and
seas combined

Years pass,
our lives like

the tides
coming in and out
but never really gone

I'm with my partner,
Avé is in the distance
the sun shining
down on them
as if they're to
leave us any minute,
I smile
wherever they go,
they are magic

She's by my side
massages my fingers
strained and paint-stained,
calluses lining them
mapping everyday
of our lives

Gaza Ranks as Top Accessible City in the World

By Car Nazzal (They/She)

For accompanying audio recording visit merajpublishing.com/inara-audio

Hey y'all I am reporting today from the Gaza International Airport! As an international artist and journalist, I have been all over the world interviewing and covering the most innovative new cultural shifts in art, architecture, and design. And it is with great pleasure that I cover this year's Gaza Accessibility Design Convention. Gaza has been at the forefront in accessibility design worldwide, being the first to rank as the most accessible city in the world by the Global Health Watch, it maintains its place as number one, though Tokyo, Japan is coming in as a close second. Many of you know that I am mixed-race and Palestinian, and I spend half the year in Al-Quds in the home my Sido built with his own two hands. While there, I was involved in historical movements and artist collectives uncovering previously stolen artifacts to research and preserve our heritage. This work has meant so much to me. AND this is the first time I have flown into Gaza International! The airport is gorgeous. It has a classic feeling built with both natural Al-Quds stone and sustainable recycled cement, with skylights and actual olive trees growing inside in mini courtyards. Directories include visual designs by Rajie Cook and codes for audio dictation. I love the amount of walking belts that make it a relaxing experience to move from one end of the airport to the other with ease, with less heavy lifting of luggage. Gaza International quite possibly has the best food court of any airport I have ever been to. The food here ranges from traditional Palestinian, with ethically lab-grown meat, to recently expanded MishMish Souq Deli for an experience where authentic Palestinian cuisine meets plant-based dining. Have you ever been to an airport and just loved the smell?! Gaza International is intoxicating with the sweet robust smell of knafeh in the air. Vendors are at the ready cooking up fresh large platters to greet travelers as they arrive or to savor before they depart. I can't believe this exists, but you can also pick up self-heating knafeh gift boxes. First you remove the syrup packets at the top, pull the small cord on the side, and the box starts to steam and heat up for five minutes, then it's ready to open, pour the syrup on top and eat! A coveted souvenir.

Right now architects, city planners, designers, press, students, and professionals have flown in via solar air, the newest form of solar flying, from all over the world to be here for the convention. The airport buzzes with anticipation. I come not just as an outside observer but as an active recipient of advanced technology developed in Gaza for those who need accessibility aids. I am dyslexic. I love being dyslexic! My dyslexia has always given me an edge as well as a different spacial and somatic perspective. My writing process involves the tool hEarMe Write tech for dictation recording and dictation editing that was invented here in Gaza. It is simple to use despite sounding complicated. The WI (willed intelligence) software accurately transcribes and makes dictating edits easy. It is like talking to a person on the other side who accurately lays the audio on the track and can understand complex directions –but it is totally secure.

Let's explore everything happening at this year's event. The Gaza Accessibility Design Convention is a month-long conference and citywide celebration, showcasing innovative architecture and design. That means three weeks packed of panels, tours, installations, workshops and exhibits showing off the world's number one accessible city. This year's program aims to explore how disability design and alternative solar energy can support each other.

Once participants arrive for event registration and gala, they are ushered into the main theater. As you enter the theater in total awe, you will notice that every single seat is accessible and customizable with large open areas for easy movement. Seats can be added or removed and there are pillows and blankets stacked as you walk in for that extra-special added comfort. The event is both in-person and streaming and there are short video vignettes playing to really help conference goers contextualize what it is like inside an accessible city and how to properly engage and navigate in Gaza. Program manager, Jad Al-Assouli had this to say, "It is really about embracing accessibility rather than viewing ability in a hierarchical mindset. Here we see all people as equals. We know that because of us, the world is changing and we want to do our part to keep inspiring change."

According to the Global Citizen Health Research Organization, 1 in 5 people worldwide has a significant disability –that's roughly 1.8 billion people and it is expected to increase. This is considered the world's largest minority. And 25% of all people will have a permanent or temporary disability within their lifetime. Palestinians are devoted to their children and future generations therefore they have taken huge strides in destigmatizing disability which is the core inspiration for the accessible city project.

Local architects went to work building a revolutionary city to adapt to the people of Gaza instead of expecting them to adapt to an unsupportive infrastructure. This completely revolutionized architecture design. "There is no one-size-fits-all due to a range of disabilities. This poses one of the biggest challenges and fun creative problem solving for designers", says Marwah Totah, renowned Palestinian architect. "We decided early in the process on the importance of openly collaborating with all firms to find the most sustainable design that supports our communities –it has been much more effective than a competitive approach." Resident blocks are dedicated to compatible communities organized to house people with different strengths so they can help each other. Homes are easily customized, for example they include hydraulic lowering counters and appliances such as stoves have knobs in the front for people who use wheelchairs. Customization is adjusted over time to support citizens as they age.

As part of the reconstruction decade and the Global Equality Resource Distribution and Reparations Act, all housing is free for people with disabilities. People who are not disabled but work as part of the compatible communities project, as well as professional caregivers are also eligible for added housing credits, making Gaza one of the most desirable places for caregivers to live.

Gaza also has the highest life expectancy for disabled people in the world, and that can be accredited to the remodeling of the healthcare system that has centered disability, physical and mental. For example, hospitals are equipped with extra large MRI machines, low hydraulic beds that go down to the floor, and customizable offices. Gaza also has a fleet of mobile medical buses making doctor house calls available to all. Doctors and staff are trained to clearly communicate directly to patients. Many of the most experienced doctors continue to practice and consult for other hospitals to ensure patients are comfortable. Many doctors themselves are also disabled, and know from experience, "When it comes to medicine, anything other than comfort is torture." Says Dr. Laila Alaqad.

Jobs are optional and available for citizens who feel called to volunteer and donate their time simply for the enjoyment it brings them. You can find them throughout the convention teaching indigenous textile weaving dyeing and tatreez techniques, crafts, and traditional food demonstrations. But also many disabled people work in tech, historical archives, as professors, as psychologists, and as animators for the Animation Studio of Palestine with plenty of remote work –making this a hub of Palestine's contemporary creative movement. Work hours are flexible allowing employees to set their hours with respect to their capacity that day.

Transportation is readily available

around the city thanks to consistent solar buses that are all wheelchair and smart chair accessible. The city also has accessible taxis which are often seen heading to the beach with people ready to enjoy the miles-long promenade. This year there is a new stop on the route, Gaza's first ever accessible pool and spa, whose grand opening coincides with this year's event! The new spa sits close to the sea with facilities both indoors and outdoors and is entirely accessible with easy lifts, ramps, and belts going into hot tubs, pools, and saunas. The building utilizes clay and wood with an echoless design shape to minimize and limit echoing sounds for those with hearing and over-stimulation sensitivities. They even have wall-mounted silent smart hairdryers! I can't wait to check out the fragrance-free gift shop full of luxurious soaps, lotions, and cosmetics. The shop is known for their diverse range of lotion textures. The spa's architect, Samar Roqaya, is especially excited about the launch. Samar happens to be deaf and signs to me via an interpreter mirror that dictates his signs out loud, "The biggest difference between our style of architecture and the rest of the world's is our goal to meet the needs of ALL people. When someone complains about something we get excited because now we have something new to invent. When someone shares what they need, we just want to help them have it. I know other countries are just starting to listen to their disabled citizens but this is what we live for. We as a people know how important it is to have our basic needs met, and it is part of our hospitality and joy to meet those needs."

Here in Gaza accessibility is not only considered for people with physical disabilities but neurodiverse folks like myself are supported too! I have been waiting all year to find out about the hEarMe Write company tech announcements. They are hosting multiple events including the release of menu readers at multiple popup cafes. But the fun and innovation don't stop there. The city has unrestricted "quiet rooms" stocked with sensory toys, pillows, and a help button if aid is needed. Quiet rooms can be found inside community buildings, spiritual centers, hotels, the grand shopping bazaar, and the airport to assist in settling down from over-stimulation. One such community center is the Gaza Neuroqueer Future Community Center which is dedicated to providing social events, education, and scholarships. The Center has a vast heirloom community garden and seed library, which is the site for many after-parties this month. Follow their updates for the full calendar.

The conference changes every year. This year it is longer than it ever has been before to allow organizers more time to be present, participate, take needed breaks, and avoid burnout. Scientist and organizer Hussam Al-Attar says "Gaza is so accessible that "disability" isn't really a word we use anymore. We have made it so all people are members of the community regardless of their earning potential. But we found that over the years we have to keep adjusting our event, keep listening to our community, and find ways for international participants to be more cohesive to our way of life because an event this size is sometimes overwhelming to our citizens." This year is expected to be the largest event in history. Al-Attar continued "Each year we continue to vote to do the conference because we know there is justice in how we innovate, and if we don't lead the way and share it –well none of us are free until all of us are free." And that's really what our Palestinian community has taught us: solidarity and how to use our privilege with purpose. The conference ends on March 22nd with a solar art installation created by Al-Attar celebrating Palestinian liberation and spirit. I hope to see you there!

Dr. Car Nazzal has a doctorate in liberation psychology and is a part-time cultural interviewer and Global Citizen, with a focus on art, psychology and Palestinian heritage. They are queer, neurodiverse mixed-race Palestinian artist and sculptor. See their artwork in museums and interviews in Queer Vogue, Palestine Times, Psych Daily and Commotion.

Art by Mishandi J. Sarhan

Fylysteen & The Evening Star

Aram Ronaldo (He/They)

*Glossary towards the end of this piece

Picture Finder Game

Count the hearts and tally them up from all the drawings

My fur is multicolored. It's usually reddish brown. But it also changes colors depending on the seasons. Brownish, whitesque, yellowsome, reddish. I'm a tanuki. Actually a rainbow tanuki. And my name is Fylysteen. Most people think I'm a fox. Or a fuzzy lap dog. I'm not though. Mistakes happen. It's okay, I'm used to it.

Today, at the moment, I'm watching the sunset. I can see part of the moon. And a few fluffy clouds. I'm letting the action inside my building complex unfold without any tanuki interruptions. The family I live with has started the preparations for their annual card playing tournament. This year's game, tarneeb.

Bethlehem Road Guest House is the name of the place. It's an inn/café/bed & breakfast combo. And apparently a convention center, from time to time. In the kitchen the three tournament weekend "menu designers," as they call themselves, are following their to-do lists. They'll have everything ready in time. They always do. The three designers are Zeez, Teez, & Sheez. Manoushé, kibbeh, tabouleh, & dolmas, that's all Zeez. Olives, pistachios, & mint tea... all Teez. And ma'amoul cookies: Sheez. I sit on a barstool by the open front door and listen in on all the sounds and chatter. All I want is some kibbeh. Gimme!!! But, I know, I'll have to wait.

"This ma'amoul wand is my magick charm," says Sheez, sitting at the kitchen table and stuffing the cookie dough with date puree, "it also makes the prettiest cookies in the world."

"Even WITH your good luck charm, you've never *won* anything," says Zeez, hovering by the bar counter and rolling the dolma filling into each grape leaf while waiting for the manoushé oven's fire to blaze.

"Teehee," giggles Teez scooping pistachios from a barell into multiple glass dishes around the room, one after another.

"So what," Sheez ignores the comment and smilingly keeps focused with stuffing momentum, "I get the ace of hearts every SINGLE time. AND the king and queen. Every time. Now that's what I call magick."

"And THEN, you lose," retorts Zeez, grabbing a wooden log and throwing it into the oven. FOOM!! The fire blazes.

"HaaaaAAAaahaaaa," Teez spills some pistachios on the floor. CLICKITY CLACK.
I turn my head to check on this scene; see if it's calm enough for me to cross the kitchen to the living room yet. But before I do, in walks Mariam from behind me covered in rose petals. She's the guest house manager. I temporarily postpone my maneuvering plans.

"Fifty people are staying here over three days and two nights. More than two hundred people will be attending the tournament in our backyard, rain or shine. And you're laughing and spilling fust'kh everywhere on the floor.

Khalass. At least, though... thank the heavens... my roses are in bloom. On the bushes, across the trellis, around the archway. Perfect timing," Mariam declares this, spinning backwards to give me a look, flicking rose petals off her wrist watch, "see?" We all see.

154

155

HONK HONK HONK!!! All of us look towards the front driveway. It's Khalty Buza.

"Khaltyyyy!" Mariam says, half-excited and half-panicked. Khalty's car is a relic of the automobilers' lifestyle splitting wide open and falling apart.

Khalty gets out of the motor vehicle with a cane and a limp. And lots of swagger..."I'mmm BACK," Khalty Buza blows a kiss directly at me.

-

We've made it to the living room. I'm drooling. There's hot kibbeh on the dining table, but I can't get it myself.

"Here," whispers Sheez and places one kibbeh ball on a teacup's saucer for me under the table. Eeep!

"SHNYARFF," I eat it in two bites. SLURP. Lip lickin' good.

"Khalty, we've been so eager to see you. How is everything in Al-Khalil?" asks Mariam.

"Great," says Khalty Buza, "And everyone is coming this weekend. Coming here," she raises an eyebrow in Mariam's direction, just checking that she is confident all around,

"They can't wait to see me win the tournament. Finally. Again."

"And your sayara? It's still big. And strong. And..." Mariam runs out of adjectives.

"Isn't this car the one that runs on hydrogen, Khalty?" asks Sheez.

"Yes. My big, strong sayara. My SHIP!!! It's a motor car that runs on hydrogen, that's correct. AND It has solar panels on the roof as well," offers Khalty Buza.

"Wow. Do they even have hydrogen refilling stations on the highway stops anymore?" ask Mariam.

"They do," Khalty continues to defend her car universe, "there are three AL-HONDA hydrogen fill-'em-ups between here and Al-Khalil. But I know, it might be time for a change. Upgrade! Another kind of fuel, perhaps, other than hydrogen power and solar power and who knows what's next."

"DONKEY POWER," yells Zeez from the kitchen.

"Fylysteen is like 50 horse power!" declares Sheez excitedly. I feel myself squinting toward the growing conversation congregation. But, after all I nod in confirmation. "Strap that harness on, and Fylysteen will dog sled your sayara over the mountains and down the freeway like the strongest pack of Alaskan huskies you've ever ridden…"
I shrug. Sure :)

I head to the couch where Mariam and Khalty Buza are sitting. Zeez and Teez keep up their hard work in the kitchen. CRACKLE goes the manoushé oven's fire.It makes me feel warm all over. Sheez takes a break, and walks over to visit in the living room with Khalty and Mariam.

Sheez has questions — enthusiastic, immediate inquiries for Khalty to answer, "I hear the farmers have many new apprentices. I wish I could be studying on a farm out there near you. Maybe one day. All the university students are totally obsessed with that stuff; farming in orchards and vineyards and groves and beehives," Sheez rambles and daydreams and we all allow it, "and lamb-sheep herding and getting the eggs from the coops of the chickens."

Yummm... eggs. Yummm... chicken.

"Yes sweetie. The young people have enthusiasm and energy aplenty. I'm very grateful to see it more than ever before," answers Khalty Buza.

Mariam shares their local news, brimming with innkeeper's pride, "We get so many more tourists than ever throughout the year Khalty. Every season continues to be abundant."

"I bet. And you're right. Things are different lately. Even my lemon tree has more lemons on it. Here's a picture," Khalty Buza shows us a picture of lemons.

"WuuuUUUUuuu," we all react aloud.

"It's good luck," says Khalty Buza.

"It's good timing," says Mariam.

"It's magick," says Sheez.

It is the later evening. I'm in the
backyard, looking up at the trellis covered in

roses of varying shades of purple blossoms. Violet? Ambrosia? Stuff like that anyway. I pick up some fallen purple-ish petals and rub them on my fur. Let's be purple. Why not. Makeup... ish.

Zeez and Teez are sitting on the ground nibbling on a large plate of dolmas with a side of olives. They're licking their fingers over their hard day's work. Khalty Buza and Mariam are each holding a small steamy glass, with a glass saucer, of mint tea. They're waiting for the tea to cool. And then they will sip it.

"I'm doing the beach bike tour," announces Zeez.

"THIS is news to *me*," says Mariam.

"Wonderful," responds Khalty.

"The one that goes from Beirut to Port Sayeed?" asks Sheez, "From beach to beach? All along the coasts? Oh my gosh, you've been wanting to do that beach bike tour since forever!" cheers Sheez.

"You'll never make it," Mariam teases.

"Teehee," Teez giggles and snorts and keeps nibbling on dolmas.

"Look," Khalty Buza directs our attention to the sky.

"WuuuUUUuu," we all look up admiringly.

"The evening star. This will guide you to your destination. Always," Khalty sips some tea from the glass SLURRRRPP, "Look up to the heavens. When we thank the heavens and the moon and the sky... we will fulfill our destinies," encourages Khalty Buza, "my destiny is to win the tournament tomorrow."

"GLEEEEP," Teez can't help it.

Khalty continues, "Your destiny is to complete this bicycle journey of the dreams you've dreamed since you were a young schoolchild."

Mariam explains, "On your bike you'll be solar powered and wind powered," and with demonstration reaches up both hands to the sky, "and star powered!"

"VyuuUUUUuuu!!!" Teez falls over with giggles. I
dare to lick one combo
olive-and-dolma-flavored finger from Teez's
hand. And I get away with it.

"Eeep," I peep.

Thanks evening star.

Khalty dictates, "The evening star was the
goddess Inanna to the Mesopotamians.
Aphrodite to the Greeks. Venus to the Romans.
Ishtar to the Assyrians. And I love them.
Worshipfulness. Just a little, anyway. Here and
there," Khalty Buza shares, and is inspired...
and is at rest in our backyard all at once.

"Food for thought. Fuel for bike," Mariam says
to Zeez.

"Maybe," decides Zeez, "Maybe."

-

Before going to my BELOVED pillowy bed, I wander once more over to the front porch. I look down. On the welcome mat is Mariam's word search puzzles booklet. I flip through. It's a handmade, multilingual issue. Some are in English, some in Arabic, and some in Armenian. Well, I suppose even adults enjoy some gaming variety. It's not all Tarneeb. I look up. I see Khalty Buza's car. A contrast, extreme, exposing the slow evolution away from technology to which Khalty's generation is loosening its tight grip. I'm with Zeez. Donkey power! Until then, this metal donkey is parked out front. The machine's shiny chrome grill and tinted windows. The cream colored gravel under its tires. The towering huge cactus right before the walkway that is a makeshift hitching post. The mountains in the distance. The olive trees on the hills. The night clouds glowing in front of the moon. And the evening star. That kibbeh was delicious. Tomorrow's gonna be chaos... Can't wait.

r	o	o	n	i	a	r	c
a	s	t	o	o	r	g	i
t	s	u	d	r	a	t	s
n	u	e	s	r	t	a	u
i	u	v	l	t	x	u	m
m	o	i	z	l	o	q	u
a	c	l	h	n	o	o	m
l	v	o	d	n	a	l	r

loquat   roots
mint   land
garlic   rain
olive   moon
music   stardust

THE
DEEDEE BINT ZEYTOUN AL HINDI
word search & spices trading co.
send and receive multiple word searches each month

THE
DEEDEE BINT ZEYTOUN AL HINDI
word search & spices trading commune-a-tree

ن	و	ب	ز	م	ز	ب	ع
م	ي	ل	ي	ر	و	ي	ا
ت	ش	م	س	خ	ف	غ	ث
ط	ج	م	ك	ة	ا	ظ	ث
ل	ر	ظ	ش	ق	ح	ب	ز
س	ة	ح	ع	ك	ت	ا	ب
ع	س	ك	ل	س	ي	س	ن
ص	د	ي	ق	ن	ف	د	و

قستق
fis'tkh

صديق sadiq
friend

كتاب
Kitab

مشمش m'shm'sh
apricot

شمس
shams

بيت beyt
house

رؤية
rouya

عسل asal
honey

شجرة
shajara

باب bab
door

pistachio
book
sun
dream

tree

170

THE
DEEDEE BINT ZEYTOUN AL HINDI
word search & spices trading co.

submit your
own word
search
creations and
swap with
others today

ꓑшрꓒ
várt rose

 uꓔꓒшE
seghán table

Eшuyшuꓑꓒy
ná básdág rabbit

ꓑшрꓒꓔy
bardéz garden

grape ꓕшꓒꓒ
khaghogh

ծꓒy zóv
sea

ꓑшꓒꓒꓕy
asdghig little star

yꓒꓒy g'rag
fire

ꓕшꓒ khagh game

ꓑꓒꓕЕꓔ
pókhenk change

Glossary

manoushé manaeesh مناقيش

Levantine pizza with za'atar on top

za'atar زَعْتَر

thyme and sumac and sesame seeds

kibbeh كبة

Levantine Bulgur and spiced meat

tabouleh تبولة

Levantine chopped salad made of tomatoes and parsley and cucumber and bulghur with lemon juice and olive oil and salt

dolmas wnⲟ̨ɗш

grape leaves stuffed with rice and tomato and onion and sometimes ground meat

ma'amoul معمول

cookies stuffed with dates and shaped with a design from a magic wand

tarneeb طرنيب

Levantine card game

tanuki

Japanese raccoon dog

fust'kh الفستق

pistachio

buza بوظة

ice cream

khalty خالتي

auntie

sayara سيارة

automobile

khalass خلص

Enough

-

Picture Finder Game

Total = 34

image 1, two: on Fylysteen's shirt and on a pocket; image 2, two: both on the ace card; image 3, fourteen: on the front door; image 4, eight: on the table cloth; image 5, three: one on each playing card; image 6, zero; image 7, one: under the honey pot; image 8, one: under the rose; image 9, two: one on the seat, one in the spokes; image 10, one: on the cactus.

Reravelling

By Haneen (He/Him)

My grandchildren, returning from a playdate
with a sunbird and its olive tree,
rush to tell me their tales.

I tell them,
Sedo, write your tales on white kites,
let them dance with the clouds,
and fall in love with the sun.

I offer them myself in watermelon slices,
and cheese sweetened with dreams.
Just like my Grandmother offered me.

I listen to them weave stories from the soil
under their fingernails,
and the rocks and leaves they collected to
show me.

Their words heal the parts of me that I never
got to know.
The child that never learnt the word diaspora,
or

how it clings onto lips like frostbite from foreign winds.

Their smiles will never know the pain of an uprooted olive tree.

"Sedo, it's your turn to tell us a story"

Unable to pick a story,
I lean back, close my eyes,
and sift through memories.

> Laying on a beach in Gaza,
> shirtless, but not exposed.
> Our sun kissing the top surgery scars on my chest.
> My fingers tracing my lineage through the sand.
> I can hear the children in the distance,
> laughing as they build sandcastles.
> Their laughter feels like a warm hug.
> Here, the sound of joy can ring as loud as it wants.
> Here, laughter is our national anthem.
>
> Resting in the shadow of an olive tree,

feeling the air flow through me while the land embraces me.

I plant my feet in the soil and search for my ancestors, the ones who planted this tree.

I thank them, and I thank the land for making me.

Visiting the Palestinian Resistance Museum.

Inside, there is an exhibit showcasing pieces from all of the separation walls that we shook and shattered with our voices.

The pieces are covered in graffiti of all the chants that we used to scream in the streets,

Symbols of our strength and unity.

Submerging myself in the sea.

We know that nature is an extension of us,

and that we are an extension of it.

So, I search for fish, in order to express my love to them,

and to a part of me.

Collecting sticks and bark to start a fire.
Gazing at the stars as we boil tea with
sage
mixed with the sound of our melodies,
and the beating heart of a tableh
brought to life by the summer breeze.

I open my eyes and find my grandchildren
waiting in anticipation,
So, I tell them a story.

The story of the magical power of our Tatreez.
A power that has been kept safe by the
whispers our ancestors hid in balls of thread,
tucked between shades of greens and reds.

I tell them about the first stitch I crossed,
how I immediately felt the magic flow through
me,
and how this magic is stitched into the fabric of
our society.

I show them thobes and tapestries,
read the patterns as bedtime stories,
and the motifs like poetry.

I promise to teach them how to thread a
needle the next time they visit me.

Photo by Maria Zreiq

Rose and Jasmine

Sonia Sulaiman (She/Her)

Zaynab's lives are plural. As they lived their present life, they would remember scenes and images, feelings, from their past. And in the world around them, signs of fate were inescapable: in museums, their own face looked back from ancient portraits, traced the outline of their soul reborn a thousand times, and that of Hasan, always just out of reach. As a child they read the story of Zaynab and Hasan, fated lovers of Palestinian folklore, a Cinderella story. They felt in their bones that the story was much more than a tale. Every time, in every age, it has been Zaynab who walked away; all but once. They had been children, imagining a home together: a green house with a brick-red roof. War came to Hasan and Zaynab. Sometimes, when they close their eyes they catch glimpses of their many lives.

Mercifully, they can't remember every detail of their immortal life. Memories pass like fragments of diamonds, and always in them they see themself in many forms. Sometimes they have been the daughter, sometimes the son—sometimes neither. And entwined in these memories is always Hasan—oblivious, unwise, filled with the deepest longing, and beautiful.

Today, they rim their eyes with kohl—the goddess Anat before a battle—and adjust their keffiyeh and agal in the mirror. It is the Day of the Key, the anniversary of the fall of empires around the world, and one of the holiest of days in Palestine. They close the door behind them, walk down the limestone steps shadowed with roses and jasmine, and take the bus to their best friend Nadia's café.

They are greeted by the pleasant thrum of people talking as they settle into their seats for the poetry open mic. Nadia is there, working the crowd. She makes a beeline for Zaynab. The host of the Green Olive Café Open Mic is elegant in her three-piece suit, her teal silk draped over her shoulders and her long dark hair streaked strikingly with grey. She smells like the qahwah she's been serving to her guests.

"It's so good to see you, Zaynab! We have quite a crowd tonight. They've come from all over Palestine, too. All to my little café."

"I mean," said Zaynab, "they used to say that we're the poets of the Arabs, y'know." They laugh.

"Are you sure you don't want to take a turn up on the stage tonight?"

Zaynab nods. "It's just not my vibe."

"Suit yourself," says Nadia and she returns to settling her patrons. Zaynab looks out over the crowd. They see flashes of traditional clothes from all over Palestine, and the diaspora too. Their gaze lingers on a particularly stunning patchwork vest in vivid red and yellow, an almost-forgotten art from the Galilee. More than a couple people, like Zaynab, combine traditionally feminine and masculine wear. Tradition is not something which binds and constricts but inspires, it is the material that the people of this new, free, Palestine, can shape. The people are no longer surviving, but thriving, growing, changing. Palestinians chart a new course nowadays, re-forming the traditional into a spectrum of new expressions, identity no longer solidified. It's an exciting time to be in Palestine.

Zaynab takes a seat near the front, their favourite spot. They take their poetry the way they take their qahwa: heady, rich, and bold. The poets are fantastic. Zaynab even recognizes a few immortals. One is a descendant of a folk saint, Amina, who used to hunt spiritual monsters across Palestine. Who knows if they're still around, but this one brings all of the fire of prophetic speech to their verses. It sends a thrill through Zaynab.

A young man walks up onto the stage. The MC introduces him as – who else? – Hasan. It's him. Really him. Zaynab stares, a mixture of old feelings pressing against their chest. He takes their breath away. Their mouth is parched, and a tension starts to build within them, slowly, as Hasan stands by the mic and raises his phone to bring up his poem for the night. He's dark, his eyes heavy-lidded and round with long lashes. This is Zaynab's prince, just as they remembered him. A sigh rises into their throat.

"This poem is called The Dream, and it's actually very personal for me," says Hasan. "I hope that it speaks to you, in the same way that it affected me when it came." He nods to the audience, standing quietly for a moment. Tenderly, he steps toward the mic and begins.

His words stun the audience with their softness. This isn't the fire of the prophets, nor the eloquence of the scholars, but a simplicity that is just as devastating. Zaynab listens. They hear each word but the more they hear, the less they are moored to reality.

"He is the noble son of the rose and the jasmine," he's saying.

"Bent to me, and his words were sweet.

A feast, life-giving water to a drought-blighted land.

His nearness flows into the cracks of me. In a dream,

I follow where he leads. Henna, mlokhia, and apple;

He feeds them all to me in language, in poetry.

I am swept up in him, this prince of men. And I wonder,

How could I be so struck by this man when I love another?

Where is the daughter of the rose and the jasmine,

And how could I ever forget her in the dark eyes of this stranger?"

"You were not wise in those days, Hasan," thinks Zaynab, remembering all those times they met and sparred with poetry, all those times Hasan failed to resonate with her words. She had come to him, as a peasant girl, poor and cherished by the mother who raised her alone. She left and came back to him as a mysterious stranger, a nobleman who visited Hasan in his palatial gardens and, again, there was poetry between them. And, again, Hasan was oblivious that the love that was kindled in him each time was the love of the same person.

"He says to me," continues Hasan. "He says to me…You have not been wise."

Blood is all there is for Zaynab, in their ears blood, in their veins fire. This is the fatal moment, isn't it? They are weary, they are yearning for an ending. "Hasan," says Zaynab, "are you finally wise?"

Hasan has finished his poem, and he looks over the crowd and sees Zaynab. He starts and locks gaze with them. As the audience shows their appreciation, Hasan stands at the mic for a moment, rooted to the spot. Then, he steps away, and Zaynab follows inexorably, as though there was a cord taut between them. In some way, there is; the strings of fate which bound them together for so many lifetimes. In silence, they pass through the crowd and out of the café together.

Outside, the two find a quiet spot under a mulberry tree, the huge, aged branches spread a shady canopy over them. Zaynab pushes Hasan against the tree and rests their arm on the trunk. "It took you long enough to grow wise, my love," they say. Hasan looks askance, and then laughs softly.

"I was confused," he admits. "Was I in love with the girl, the boy...The mighty lord who visited me in my palace, or the young woman living in poverty who lost her golden sandal? Turns out, it was always you. I kept reaching for you, in every form you took. I thought, 'I love the girl—but I also love this boy...How can that be? Surely, I have to be in love with one, don't I?' I was so unwise not to see it. Of course, love doesn't have to be constrained like that. How could I not have known?"

Zaynab sighs, "just thinking about it makes me tired."

"I know. I tried, Zaynab. I tried so many ways to...make things right. It was like there was a current that always drew me away from you. We missed each other in so many lifetimes for such trivial reasons, or it was the Occupation. I joined the Resistance and that also took me away from you. There was always something—"

"Yeah," says Zaynab. "Something was always missing in the equation, somehow." She looks over at Nadia. "I think we have a good chance of making things work this time around."

Over time, Zaynab comes to reflect that their country is ancient, as their souls are both ancient, and young, in this freedom that is finally theirs. And when they come together, it is to discover the potentiality of all that love could mean. Instead of the fairy tale driving them onto the rocks, and circumstances drawing them apart again, they are truly free to know themselves and their desires. In exploring what 'love' means to them, they find something else: unhurried and quiet, a long proposal of mutual, intimate friendship. There are more kinds of soulmates, it turns out, than just romantic ones and more that can draw people together than the intricately woven strings of a fated love.

One day, Hasan and Zaynab walk the old city together. "I think we've finally solved the equation," says Zaynab as they turn to watch Nadia approaching, her trailing a rolling suitcase. "It's only a day trip," they say as Nadia pulls up. "You won't need all that just to go to the beach."

"Oh, it's just the sea to you, that's not how I see it. I'm not here only because I need to keep an eye on you." Zaynab elbows Nadia.

"Someone has to be the responsible one in our trio," agrees Hasan. Nadia smiles.

"You're growing on me," she says. "Now, are you going to keep talking or...?" She hoists her bag into the car. Zaynab and Hasan pile in after her. Life is sweet, beautiful, and bright in the azure sky. The hills give way to the Mediterranean. They stay out in the waves and the shore so late, but there are no regrets. There is plenty of time to make something new between them, a kind of love they haven't tried in all of their lives.

Art by Mishandi J. Sarhan

I love being the rain over Falasteen

Ali Khader (He/Him)

Poem 1:

I am the man and the earth
With each footfall, a new birth
feet and mud colliding
Uranus and Gaea intertwining
Pin-balling down the twisted path
Grateful for this honey comb scented, sun-ray
bath
Grabbing at grape vines along the way
wind breeze and olive trees
I smell the seas
Nosediving into midday with ease
As I pass the trees that my father planted
I remember the day our ship had landed
That day I was eleven
A miracle they had said
They had taken down the final hydra head
And now we sleep once more on palestinian
beds

Flash to the present

towards my neighbor's place I run

A parcel of good news rolled up on my tongue

Oh this will be so much fun!

Today I am twenty-seven

Living between the seas in heaven

And today I learned that my sister is welcoming another

A Palestinian heart beating in a palestinian womb

she will become a mother

My neighbor lives atop a hill

The house right at the very tip of its bill

I knock thrice and little Noor answers the door

My neighbor's youngest of four

How does that one song go? I think

"And her eyes, my little bird, you'd call them two cups filled with coffee.

your eyes are so black and oh so pretty"

She giggles at my attempt at the lullaby

"Shoo shoo, my butterfly"

I hear my neighbor chuckle

One long warm embrace later

We're in the garden

The sun's rays harden

His hand feels right in mine

He tells me about his week

How his art is beginning to seek

New waves of palestenian consciousness

"I can see the peak"

His lips in a grin, a study on playfulness

I plant a kiss on his cheek and watch it grow

A nursery of flowers blooming on his cratered skin

I let his words flow

The sun somehow is already about to set

I let my neighbor go

I am so happy

As I walk back towards my little life

I am so loved

By the coffee eyed people

I am so safe

My community is family

My family is community

I will always remember the day I told my neighbor my sister was pregnant

Poem 2:

Now that we are here, Falasteen
take the time to ask yourself

Why is my body my body?
why is my hair my hair?
This smile, those teeth
The never ending eyelashes,
Where do they come from?
framing two balls of chocolate-covered
marshmallow treats
Beneath densely forested brows
Why this skin?
That smells of fresh biscuits that warms in the
sun
Somewhere between toiling and rolling sand
dunes and raw smooth limestone
Ah
I ask myself these things looking up at your
orange sky
At my cheeks becoming the color of your
summer peaches
At the call to prayer in the distance

At the curves of my naked waist

At the bird receiving gifts from your soil

At the coarse hair that grows on my chest and
trails down to the space between my thighs

As green fingertips whisper faintly with the wind

Caressing my cheek, my arm, my bare feet

The electric current in your dirt tethering my
soul in place

As I hover two inches from the earth

Ah

Fossils and shells of a rich history sleep under a
thin layer of crystalized honey...

your honey, dripping into parted lips

Now look side to side

On your vast fragrant earthen body

And see

Someone right beside us

Why is his body his body?

Why is his hair his hair?

And once and for all

Why did it take so long for me to ask?

For me to wonder?

The magic that created me created all of us

It is in me and in you, Palestine

It is the pearl softly resting in the fossa where

our heart once was

At the center of the universe

A heart that now sits in our skull caressing minds

Like the mother we miss

Like the kiss we share

Right then and there

under your dawn sky

Ah!

In you, I see me

In your eyes I see home

I dress you slowly, Falasteen

And when I catch your memory in a

photograph, out my window, or in the mirror

I smile

Poem 3:

Mama has been singing

She began trading in gold ankle bracelets
once more
Olive tree heaven
once more
Falasteen once more.
handmade brick ovens
Waft scents of taboon bread
Over Anzah...
oh Anzah! she sings
On her streets your eyes flood
with spilled golden sesame seeds and zaatar
Like chips of gold on horse-tracked dirt roads
Her current occupation: Teaching children
how to craft
Cypress tree necklaces
And speak their mother tongue.
Speak it loud and proud for you are
palestenian, she proclaims
Your blood is fire and your heart beats like a
Doumbek drum!

smell citrus showers in these palms

For these calloused hands, once wielded by
your kin, laid brick by brick Al-Aqsa itself!

Her hand moves from holding mine

Dances towards Earth

Planting yet another olive seed

 in nature's heart

By her side I finally say,

Rather I whisper,

Or maybe just think:

I am free

Our bodies are rested

Minds not weary

Our code is alive

Our code is real

I dream of sweet things

Of wonders and promises lining my cells like the
DNA I'm learning to love

For I have studied these nucleotides ending in
olive branch telomeres

Under electron microscope

I watch them

grow tall and strong

Dip them in honey

Once for each year of remembrance I carry

Each feather on my wings

an ancestor yet to be born.

My Falasteen, I say

my lips curl up towards the heavens

Like half eaten date ka'ak

I wrap my arms around my busy mother

I am here

And so are they

My grandma and great grandma and great
great great grandma

singing "Safar Barlek"

But this time, with the memory of

What comes next

"To return free, ya mama

How lucky are we

Really free, ya mama"

Falasteen

As in Ali

Me

As in Ana

You

As in Inti

Us

As in ihna

We are Free

As in horiyah!

Poem 4:

A collection of words that all mean the same thing:

Mother

Matter

Mama

Earth

Safety

Love

Falasteen

Nature

Kindness

Home

Heart

Fight

Compassion

Protect

Connectedness

Selfless

Giving

Nurture

Free

A collection of words that all mean the same thing, part 2:

Falasteen

Freedom

Friend

Unity

Community

Kites

Refaat Alareer

Kanafe

Music

Soul

Tatreez

Liberation

Musakhan

Blood

Skin

Rain

Art by Mishandi J Sarhan

Poem 5:

Three shooting stars in the night sky

one after the other

I look right at my mother

Mouths and eyes wide

Like jam jar lids

A sea of bodies stills

In awe at a miracle

music and strobe lights remain sightless and unaware

"Did that just happen"

A guest whispers

"Heaven really said 'mabrook'"

Another laughs

I turn to my now-husband

He smiles

Our hands intertwined

"God is real, my love"

Time resumes

the sea begins to groove

Ripples making ripples

My white suit

Glistens under the moon

My sister

The tireless wedding general

pinches my cheek

On her way to the cliff's edge

Overlooking the salty Dead Sea

She did what I asked

This truly is a spectacle

I bet she struck a deal with god

Erupting the heavens

Just for us

This night sky we share

Jerusalem orange wine

Numbing my fingertips

I paint the air with laughter

As I think of what comes after

Poem 6:

Sometimes

somewhere

somehow

I become a bird

Sunbird on a clear day

A national bird

I scout ants

Living and thriving hardworking ants

Now and then

I am also the gazelle

Legs long and slender

Doing what gazelles do

I eat and rest

Eat and rest

Often these palestinian children

Come up to me with leaves and stems

So I nibble at them from their palms, of course...

And then I rest

But you know

My favorite thing to be

Most of all

My favorite thing to be

The rain

I am each raindrop

Each molecule

Each atom

The sound I make against their windows

The memories I conjure on a long drive

One time I saw her standing there

As I poured

Palms facing the sky

A kufiyeh over her russett curly hair

And a smile on her full lips

I hear the prayers on their witty tongues

In their mischievous hearts

Welcoming me in with laughter

The best thing about being the rain?

Becoming the fertile earth

The color of dirt ever slightly more

Vibrant

Alive

Free

And that's when I become

Ever

Green

Grape leaves you roll

Flower gardens you stroll

The trees

and between them the breeze

The chlorophyll

Your houses on the hills

And at some point

I turn into you

The cytoplasm in your cells,

The blood in your veins,

The pool which suspends your brain

And when you kiss one another

I become all of you

And you become all of me

Oh I love it so much

I love being the rain

Over

Falasteen

Poem 7:

There are two days to every soul

I tell the onlookers,

the day we are born

Our birth day

We celebrate

The milestones of each day

Threads that connect us

Each day a miracle

Thank you for being here with me

Friends

Family

My partner

Community

Spirit

Palestine

Today I learned something I didn't know
yesterday

Tomorrow I will partake in the mundane
spectacular

I will carry all this gold

Golden threads with me

In my chest

Filling the spaces between my ribs

So that every inhale

Every exhale

(breathe in)

(breathe out)

Is a reminder of how rich I am

So rich in fact that if I picked each golden
string

I could sit at a loom and weave

A sweater

That's about 20,000 stitches

20,000 times where my universe collided with yours

I would not subtract a single day

I would not subtract a single thread

Now I am at my death bed

My death day

The other day that is

As inevitable as birth

And I hold my soft golden sweater against my cheek

I can't wait to show this to Him

My creation

All of you by my side

How lucky are we to experience this life

How lucky are we to have met

I will share with the night sky the golden threads of all of us

I will whisper in god's ear that I lived each day on Falasteen

Fully

Fell in love in Falasteen

Lived in Falasteen

I breathe each day with you

I loved each day with you

Lay me down on the palestinian grass

Let my universe collide with the earth one last time

as they become one

My People Shall Love

رند (She/Her)

Freedom is calling

I saw it in your eyes

Closer towards us

You told me with your smile

So much between us

Rivers and seas

Knowing that one day

They'll bring you close to me

I read your poem every time I miss you. I've spent years reading your poem. Paper tattered and torn, yearning for its smooth edges in the palm of your hand, the way it felt when you first gave it to me.

Our tree is still here. Where I carved your name into a heart, where you carved yours into mine. Next to the others.

Are they still here? Do they visit this tree too?

I want you to know that I kept our promise. The children are performing a play they wrote about our love today. It feels like the first day I met you.

We were both 12, caught between the final moments of girlhood and the rest of our lives.

"Do you like to read?"

"Sometimes." I couldn't remember the last time I picked up a book that wasn't assigned in school.

"I wrote this essay about my favorite fantasy book that's opening in theaters next week." You walked me to your bedroom and showed me your latest works displayed on the wall. "I write my own stories too,"

I asked what you liked to write about.

"Love," without pause or hesitation.

I've always heard songs, movies, and poetry describe falling in love in similar ways. Where just hearing the person's name spins you out of reality. The dimensions I've traveled, bewildered by the infinite since you told me yours.

Your first gifts to me—the knots in my stomach and the series of electric shocks gripping my chest, all bittersweet outcomes in the taste of your gaze; the pain of the longing, the joy of its suspense.

You would sneak into my room and ask if I wanted to go to your favorite spot at the beach. I didn't care about anything else. I wasn't afraid of anything with you and I would've gone anywhere you asked. Especially if it meant we were together.

Walking there was my favorite part. We always took the same footpath curated by us and no one else, but every time we went, it felt like a new place.

Time traveling through our desires past, present and future, we confessed our dreams to the sky.

Freedom is calling

I saw it in your eyes

Closer towards us

You told me with your smile

So much between us

Rivers and seas

Knowing that one day

They'll bring you close to me

That morning was the first time you held my hand. I retrace this memory against the feeling of your fingertips tracing mine every time I miss you. I've spent years retracing your fingertips against my own memory.

In the salty breeze of the sea, I can still taste your skin from our last night together.

Your book was recovered and I learned about how you dedicated your days to the children.

It doesn't feel like you ever left. You respond to my calls in the echoes of the wind and I smile now, remembering it all, watching it play out by the same children.

"Nothing has the power to separate me from my journey to your heart." The play concludes with your oath to the sea the last day we spent here together. The children take their bows as the sun sets on this same horizon that holds our dreams.

You kept your promise in the grace of the sea,

I kept mine on the shores of our land you freed for me.

I blink, grateful for our love, our love, our love. Me and you. Me and Her. Me and everyone that's home.

Art by Mishandi J. Sarhan

Love, Land and the Sea

By Lama (they/them)

Glossary with Arabic words & phrases at the end of this piece

As dawn breaks, the sun emerges from the horizon, casting its golden rays across the indigo canvas of the sky. I savor the familiar ritual of sipping coffee on the rooftop perch. Twenty-five years of Friday mornings in Maadi, Cairo watching the beautiful sunrise's hues painting the sky with a palette of golden yellows and soft pinks, casting a mesmerizing glow over the city. Still, nothing could rival the ethereal beauty of daybreak over the fig-laden branches of my grandparents' home in Alma, Safad. My mind is dancing with anticipation, wandering, thinking about journeying with Toyo, in just a couple of hours to Gaza, Palestine before heading to Alma. It is our first time back in Palestine as a married couple, and I am so excited.

I love journeying together throughout the year to one another's communities. I would not have known four years ago when we met at the African teachers union amidst the vibrant bustle of Lagos, Nigeria that we would be here. When I met Toyo I couldn't help but be captivated by the way she spoke of her ancestral soil, her words infused with a deep-rooted reverence for the earth. We got to know one another through traveling and exchanging knowledge and resources with one another's communities. I grew more and more in love with Toyo's wisdom and gentle spirit. Our bond flourished through tender care for our own and each other's communities, it is the foundation to our relationship.

Our year, guided by the seasons, is spent across Lagos, Maadi, and Alma. We spend the winter months in Lagos with Toyo's family to attend yam farming season helping plant yams in the community farm.

Spring calls us to Maadi, to work with my father, Hassan, on boats in the Nile transporting traded goods from lower Egypt to upper Egypt. Toyo, being a brilliant wood worker, crafts the boats we work. Both of us being children of great sailors we sail away up and down the Nile all spring. The summer takes us to Alma, Safad to where we spend it with Sido and Jeddo, caring for the village's fig trees and working with mama in the village school. Toyo teaches math and I teach physics and poetry.

In the languid transition from spring to summer, amidst the whispering breeze that carries the promise of sun-kissed days, we bid farewell to Maadi. It is time to set our sights on the Palestinian shores. My heart brims with glee, I am so eager to be amidst the myriad wonders of Gaza—the crystalline sea, mesmerizing sunsets, and the joys of biking through the city with Toyo. Unable to wait any longer, I rush downstairs to wake Toyo up. My heart quickens at the thought of embarking on this trip, it is just as exciting every time. Toyo is looking angelic in deep sleep, I hate that I have to wake her up, but it is time to get going. I gently kiss her on the cheek, "Sabaho yalla habibi, the sea is waiting." She opens her beautiful eyes slowly and stretches like a cat with a big smile across her face. Sleepy and excited, she stumbles to the washroom to get ready for the day.

I slip into my swimsuit and shorts, and gather the last things we need to pack. I notice from the corner of my eye Toyo scrambling looking for something, she is pacing back and forth from her closet to the laundry room scattering everything around. I quickly realize what is happening. "Habibi, your travel overalls are right here ironed ready for you." Toyo smiles and quickly jumps into their overalls ready to take off.

All done packing, I zip up the bags and Toyo packs the snacks and medication "Nada my love, all set and ready to go?" Toyo calls. "Yes hayati, yalla." We stroll to the bus stop and catch the bus to the train. Toyo is beaming, I love seeing her so excited. We sway side to side as the bus driver zooms through the bustling streets of Cairo, hurrying to get to the train stop. We arrive just on time, and grab window seats across from one another, uninterrupted access to stunning views. "I love this train ride so much, the scenery is so enchanting." I hold her warm hands "I told you, there is nothing quite like our beautiful Mediterranean."

Toyo, alarmed, "Nada, habibi are you okay; your hands are freezing, did you eat?" I giggle in guilt "I actually forgot, I am jittery and really hungry now that you mention food!" Toyo sighs "I just knew it, you get excited and forget everything else. Here, let's have some breakfast." She takes out my favorites from the food bag she so carefully prepared and in classic Toyo behavior stuffs a date in their mouth. "To warm your stomach up for the food, it is sunnah!" We both dig in, munching on fatayer, chips, foul sandwiches and wash it down with Asab.

Bellies full and minds relaxed, we wonder at the beautiful landscapes beyond the window. I look over and Toyo, calmed by the rhythm of the train, slips into a nap. The journey to Gaza unfolds as a tapestry of urban sprawls, verdant farmlands, and undulating desert vistas. Toyo eventually awakes and I seamlessly weave stories with the shifting tableau outside our windows, painting vivid pictures of my childhood memories in the Mediterranean's beaches, my family's chaos, and breathtaking sunsets.

As we traverse into Gaza, the landscape transitions from the arid grandeur of the desert to the captivating allure of the Mediterranean coast. The tantalizing scent of saltwater permeated the air, heralding a day filled with the symphony of crashing waves and the succulence of ripe fruits. I squeeze Toyo's hands to check if she is ready and awake. Toyo settles in her seat ready to get off the train. As soon as the train settles into the station, I feel Toyo jumping off her seat. Unable to wait, she rushes to grab the bags and get off the train. I stumble and follow her out of the train.

I text Samer, my cousin, to let them know we are here, they immediately text me they are outside. We exit the station to see Samer in their orange cap and a purple summer dress surrounded by all the cousins. The eager anticipation of my cousins, rushing forth to envelop us in warm embraces, heralded the beginning of a beautiful day. We are received by the harmonious melody of the sea and the inviting embrace of sun-kissed sands. The cousins take all of our bags and munch on some of our snacks, rushing away to the family's umbrella at the shoreline.

My heart leaps with uncontainable joy at the sight of my family. I hold Toyo's hands in adoration of her infectious laughter as she playfully tugs me towards the crescent of chairs arranged by the water's edge. As we approach my aunties, uncles, and Sido and Jeddo, they all rise from their seats and envelop us in a tidal wave of hugs and kisses. The air is charged with palpable excitement, the anticipation of reuniting us with the family for the first time since our wedding.

The aunties immediately start reminiscing about the beautiful day. It was a mere six months ago and still lingering in all our memories. It was a breathtaking affair, set against the backdrop of the serene shores of Taba, Egypt caressed by the gentle waves of the Red Sea. The sun dipped below the horizon, casting a golden glow over the beach, and the festivities began. I could see my aunties' eyes sparkling with the magic of that unforgettable evening as they thought back to the day.

The rhythm of Palestinian folk music intertwined seamlessly with the pulsating beats of Afrobeats and the infectious energy of mahragant. The dance floor became a stage for cultural fusion, as guests moved to the eclectic blend of melodies. Each step was a celebration. The air reverberated with the vibrant sounds of African and Arab drumming, infusing the night with life and joy. A night that has forever been etched in our collective memory. It was everything I dreamt of and more and everyone can't help but feel the same joy they felt then when recalling the day.

I look over to my side to see Sido and Toyo chatting, the two have a tradition of exchanging knitted goodies every time they see each other. Sido pulls out a beautiful burgundy cardigan he knitted for Toyo. Toyo smiling ear to ear holding the cardigan close, "Thank you so much, Sido, I love the color, it is the perfect size too." Toyo turns and brings out an olive green blanket she made for him and his eyes tear up with joy. I hear his loud and energetic voice excitedly say "Thank you, ya amar," clutching the blanket. "It's perfect for the cool summer evenings here." He has a special place in his heart for Toyo, their bond is so sacred.

I'm already hungry again and inhaling Amto Fawziyeh's ma'moul and fatayer. I wash it down with the sugar cane juice I brought with me from Cairo. Jeddo, squats down, fans the coal, preps the grill, and then calls to me, pointing to a cooler where he has figs, watermelon and grapes just for me. I immediately dive in without hesitation, "Thank you ya albi, I missed Falastin's fruits so much."

Sido rushes and interrupts us eating and chatting, insisting it is time to dive into the sea. Unable to say no to the love of his life, Jeddo designates Samer to watch over the grill and he follows Sido to the sea. I can see him looking at Sido with love pouring in his eyes, watching his spouse run towards the water. I am so glad Sido beat me to it, because Jeddo would never ask him to wait and I was ready to be in the sea. Overjoyed, I drag Toyo to follow and we make our way to the water's edge. Toyo hesitates, worried that the waves may be a bit too high. I try to reassure her, but only Jeddo's steadying hand will convince her to join. Toyo takes his offered hand. He sighs "We are part of the sea, ya Jeddo, it knows how to hold us; let the waves carry you in." He gently guides her through the waves, hopping through one by one. They make it past the high waves; reassured by Jeddo, Toyo dives right in with him.

Trusting that Toyo is in good hands, I swim ahead with Sido, diving into the inviting waves saying "ta da da dadada ta da da daa" matching the waves' vibrations. Sido looks over at Toyo and shares "the sea is where all prayers are answered, ya habeeba, pray and ask for all that your heart is calling for." He calls on the vastness of the sea to bring an abundance of joy and softness to our life. We wiggle in the water like fish and unbridled joy washes over me as I take in this moment.

Two people approach the water. I squint my eyes trying to figure out who they are. Toyo giggles, making fun of my terrible sight and confirms it is my parents. Laila and Hassan dive, giggling and humming to the song of the waves dancing. This is my favorite part of the trip: I get to swim with Baba and Mama into the deep crystal blue, our sea tradition. They dive right in and make their way over and I rush their greetings "yalla Baba lets go, I have been waiting for you to get here to go in." Toyo looks at me, giving me the "you better be careful" eyes. We start swimming like fish in the water, my heart syncing with the rhythm of every wave and stroke.

Baba notices Mama swimming behind us. The three of us make our way into the sea till land turns to a speck and the lifeguard starts whistling in the megaphones warning us to not go any further and we heed their call. All we can see is where the sky kisses the water. With every splash and every dive, we revel in the rhythm of the Mediterranean, our hearts entwined with the timeless beauty of our home. We float with our faces up in the same spot. In the embrace of the sea, amidst the laughter and the crashing waves, I feel an indescribable sense of serenity—a deep gratitude to be in Palestinian waters.

Nothing makes me feel at home quite like swimming deep into the sea; I feel so lucky to have been swimming on the same stretch of the shore—West in Egypt's Sahel and East in Gaza's Bahr. The sound of waves and chirping birds surround me, all thoughts fade away as my body blends with the ocean blue, and the universe whispers songs of joy, protection, and ease. My heart has never felt so light and full at the same time. Daydreaming I almost drift away until Baba notices and calls on me to swim back. Baba and Mama hold me close, all three of us cycling in the water, just like when I was a kid.

Mama hears my stomach growling and gestures it is time to head back. She starts humming with the waves and guides us back to the shore. Toyo and the grandparents had already made their way out, back to the umbrella. The cousins see us coming out of the water and rush over holding up towels. We curl up into them and walk over to the umbrella. Baba, in classic manner, lays out a dry towel on the sand in the sun and lays down to dry and I follow laying right next to him as Jeddo and Toyo prep the food together. Toyo does not like cooking, but she loves helping Jeddo by the grill, the smell of grilled fish reminds her of the grilled fish she ate growing up in Lagos.

The family gathers on the sand and indulges; Amto urges the kids to eat all their food. The spread includes grilled fish, calamari, spicy gazan salad packed with all the chili it can take, hummus, tabbouleh, and an array of seafood that were all eaten with fresh bread.

Sido recalls stories of her early married days with Jeddo in the village before they had all their kids "Subhanallah, who would have known that we would all be sitting just a few kilometers away from where your Jeddo and I met for the first time? Back then, we could not spend a day like this in Gaza, but we knew this day would come. Alhamdulella for the gift of life, for the sea, the food, and you, jewels of my soul." As I listen to him I can feel joy settle in my chest and my eyes tearing up.

I look over to the shore, taking in the view of the sun dancing towards the sea, casting a warm glow over the beach. Samer gets up and pulls me up with him and calls for the rest of the cousins to join, their laughter harmonizing with the waves. We rise in dabkeh, our feet moving in unison to the beat of the oud Ammo Yasser is playing. I can feel my feet fluttering through the sand, as the ground

234

dances to our beat. Samer looks beautiful as the orange of the sky reflects off their skin; they were glowing in bliss.

As evening embraces the beach, we start to slowly make our way from Gaza to Alma, our hearts full of beautiful moments and bellies stuffed with food. We waddle sleepy and blissful to the train. We get on and slowly journey through the fading light, with the grandparents sharing stories of their childhood in Alma's stone-paved streets and the latest village gossip. Sido goes on about Amo Hamed's new bakery and the aroma of freshly baked bread that has been wafting from their ovens all over the street. It sounds like a dream, there is nothing like waking to the smell of fresh bread filling the air.

The landscapes transition once again, this time from the coastal beauty of Gaza to the rolling hills and olive and fig groves of Alma. The village unveils itself like a painting on the canvas of time. The stone houses adorned with vibrant bougainvillea, and the jasmine flowers dancing with the wind in celebration of the family's arrival. The air was infused with the scent of thyme and the comforting familiarity of home.

We finally arrive to the house, Jeddo's voice softly asks if we would like to eat something before bed. Tired and sleepy I gesture with my hands on my belly that I am full to the brim and ready to float in sleep. We carry the bags up to our rooms and quickly fall asleep, drifting like waves into dreams.

As the first rays of dawn pierce through the darkness, and the scent of bread breaks through morning mist I open my eyes. Eagerly welcoming the arrival of a new day, I get right out of bed and get ready to head downstairs. I tiptoe down the stairs and, careful not to wake Toyo and Sido up, I make my way to the kitchen. To my delight Jeddo is, as expected, up early tending to the mint and sage plant pots by the window. I meet his warm smile and the comforting aroma of freshly brewed coffee. "Sabaho," he leans in, kissing me softly

on the forehead before pouring me a
steaming pot of coffee.

In this moment, surrounded by the gentle hum
of nature awakening outside and the familiar
sights and sounds of our home, I can feel the
cool morning breeze caressing my face gently.
It's as if time stands still, allowing me to fully be
present in the beauty of this place—made all
the more beautiful with the presence of Jeddo.
This is our sacred morning time together. With
each sip of coffee, the energy of the land
infuses our very being. The energy here
grounds me in a sense of calm and belonging
that transcends time and space. I gaze out at
the fields of green stretching out before me
and I cannot help but feel grateful to share my
favorite part of the day with my favorite
person.

We sit on the balcony watching the sun rise
over the village; the birds chirping and the
smell of fresh bread takes over filling the air. As
Jeddo reminisces, his voice carries the essence
of the land itself—the symphony of olives being

picked at harvest time, the heady fragrance of ripe figs hanging heavy on the branches, the rhythmic sound of water trickling through the soil to nourish the thirsty earth. To him, every sight, every sound, every scent was a testament to the resilience and vitality of Alma, a place where the past and present coexist in perfect harmony.

I long to freeze this moment in time, to etch it into my memory for all eternity. But the distant hum of the village, the smell of bread teasing my growling stomach is sign enough that breakfast is due. Together, we make our way back inside, to find Sido already kneading the dough and Toyo setting up the table. Jeddo has other plans for the family and calls Toyo to help him set up a table on the balcony instead, so we can eat in the sun. I can see Toyo's breath taken away by the view from the balcony, the mountains looming in the distance and the fig trees swaying in the gentle breeze.

As Toyo follows Jeddo to the balcony, they collect some fresh olives, thyme, sage, and tomatoes from the garden. The aroma of the fresh herbs mingles with the sweet smell of the ripe tomatoes, filling the air around us. Meanwhile, I carry trays of manaeesh to Amo's bakery with the cousins. The smell of akkawi cheese, Za'atar, olive oil, and Muhammara waft through the streets, drawing in people from far and wide. I give Hana the baker figs, Za'atar and sage from our garden and she helps us take the manaeesh out of the oven and back to the house.

We sit around the table, enjoying the freshly baked manaeesh, the warm sun, and each other's company. Jeddo asks "Where are Laila and Hassan, have you seen them?"
Sido replies "They probably went on their usual morning walk; they should be back shortly."
Toyo, lost in admiration of the view from the balcony, notices two people approaching from a distance "Ah I see them Jeddo, they are here!" My parents return from their morning stroll through the village, the warmth of the

rising sun illuminating their faces. I see them carrying a woven basket filled with plump dates. "Ahla Sabah ya Hilween." Mama greets everyone, and settles herself next to me. Hungry, her eyes twinkling at the sight of the fresh labneh, she asks me "Mama, can you pass the Labneh?"

"Did you sleep well, Habibi?" she asks warmly. Nodding and passing her the labneh, "Very well, Mama, thank you. After a day at the sea and the fresh air here I slept like a baby." Baba chuckles, taking a seat beside Mama. "That's the magic of Alma, isn't it? Nothing quite like it." I nod in agreement, tearing off a piece of warm bread to stuff my face with foul. "There is nothing like Alma's food; everything tastes better here. Something in the soil and the air are different."

Mama's gaze softens watching me with a sense of pleasure swelling in her chest. "We're blessed. To be surrounded by family and the beauty of our land is a gift from Allah, Allah yehmeekom w yese'dkom ya mama." Baba nods in agreement, his eyes sparkling with affection. He reaches for a date from the basket replying "Laila habibi yalla finish your food, so you are all fueled up to head to the gardens with Ammy."

Jeddo giggles "Not before tea with the dates you've brought first. No need to rush into the fields just yet, my son. Take your time." With that, they settle into their chairs, enveloped in the soothing fragrance of freshly brewed tea and the delightful sweetness of the dates. It feels like time stretches and slows down, like a lazy cat basking in the warmth of the sun.

Full and ready for a walk, I rise from my seat "Habibi, Toyo, let's go for a walk?" I extend a hand to my beloved wife. With her belly extending in front of her and a satisfied smile, she pulls on my hand to get up. The morning sunbathes the village in a radiant glow, casting everything in golden hues as we stand at the threshold of Alma. In this moment, our hearts feel intertwined with the very spirit of the land, pulsating with the murmur of the trees. Toyo shares, "Our relationship has been a journey of realizing that home isn't just a dot on a map, but a living, breathing entity that weaves my story with yours. I fell in love with Alma through your eyes, through your heart. It is crazy how familiar this place feels for me." I hug Toyo, I am always in awe of how she is able to put words to feelings so beautifully. I run out of words to describe the comfort and joy of existing with ease in the quiet embrace of nature with the love of my life. It is a gift to be anchored in each other's legacies, bearing witness and honoring the present while forging our path together, in love and dedication to our lands and people.

Art by Summar

Glossary

Love, Land and the Sea - in order of appearance

- **sabaho** - good morning
- **habibi** - my love
- **yalla** - let's go
- **sunnah** - Muslims follow certain habits and action in the way the Prophet Mohammed PBUH had performed. They are seen to promote our overall well being and balance in resemblance to the prophet.
- **fatayer** - Savoury Pies typically filled with cheese, spinach, a red pepper paste or thyme (Za'taar).
- **foul** - Fava bean dish that is very popular across South West Asian and North Africa and largely eaten for breakfast
- **Asab** - sugarcane juice
- **taba** - A city in Egypt and on the border with Palestine, the Red Sea is the most gorgeous there and the waters are both Palestinian and Egyptian waters.
- **ma'moul** - Palestinian cookie, typically filled with dates or nuts. This specific one is made by Nada's aunt.
- **albi** - My heart and endearing term used to express love.
- **Sahel** - Shoreline

- **Bahr** - Sea
- **tabbouleh** - A Levantine salad made of parsley, bulgur, tomato and onion.
- **Amo** - uncle
- **Za'atar** - is thyme spiced and roasted in a traditional Palestinian way, it's used very often as part of various Palestinian dishes, as well as, eaten on its own with bread and olive oil.
- **manaeesh** - Palestinian savoury baked goods filled with cheese, thyme (Za'ataar), Res pepper paste (Mubammra) and much more.
- **Ahla Sabah ya Hilween** - Most beautiful morning, lovelies
- **Labneh** - A Levantine strained yogurt dip commonly
- **Allah yehmeekom w yese'dkom ya mama** - May Allah protect you and bring you joy.
- **Ammy** - my uncle

Art by Summar

The Guardian of Falasteen

Yaffa AS (They/She)

The particles of sand tickle my feet as I glide on Gaza beach. I giggle, enjoying the self made tickling sensation not for the first time. The laughter around me makes me laugh, feeling the setting sun on the skin of those around me and I mimic the sensation.

In the distance two hijabis kiss, the sun disappearing and appearing between them as if they are the sun. I smile watching their entire lives unfold in one eye and their smiles in the other. Near them a child creates and stomps a sand castle, time is of no consequence to me and sometimes I speed things up accidentally.

Rewind and repeat, I see the kiss again, the child playing. They look up towards me, as if they could see me, but I am invisible in every way except energetically. I bow to them and they shudder and then smile, the sun shining against their blue black skin.

I walk off, flitting between time and space, witnessing every moment in every life. People-watching is my favorite.

I watch as the sea thrashes against the treehouse cities along the coast tens of miles away. Silly humans, believing elevation will save them. I inhale the sea through the trees and exhale it back into the sea that was once named the center, and in many ways it still is. I see it expanding, claiming the coasts and growing into the ocean it was always meant to become. I see its joy, the joy of the people recognizing self-actualization in movement, in being one with it.

I walk back, to children running, drawn to laughter right before cries. A child falls, scraping their knees, but the other children are too far off to notice, they are alone, their cries echo in the distance, it will take 444 seconds for someone to find them. I step towards them, though I don't need to, and although I don't know how it feels to be held I can see the feeling reaching them, first in their eyes relaxing–their eyelids open and close like a butterfly's wing–their face smooths, and although they continue crying it is as if they are held by a loved one as they do so.

I move on before they find them, my work is done here.

***

My gold chains chime with the wind as the boat glides in the sea. The fishers laugh and joke with one another in between bouts of silence as they catch the fish needed to feed their village today. The wedding later will be filled with bass and bream. Fish is sacred, eaten during festivities in an otherwise mostly vegetarian diet as the world replenishes its natural resources.

I toy with the current, allowing the boat to move towards the fish and the fish towards the boat, like long lost lovers waiting to meet.

***

They're writing on a typewriter, like they do most mornings, their books sprawled around their office like children unwilling to leave their parents' side. They don't know it yet, but they soon will get a message saying their train time has changed, they will now depart three hours earlier.

They stop mid sentence when it comes through, not knowing that they will never finish that sentence.

They get up hurriedly, stressed and yet motivated and open to receiving the joy of change. Their bags are more packed than they remembered, everything they need exactly where they need it to be, not where it was. They are out the door, a car awaits them outside, their wheelchair easily fitting inside.

The train departs two minutes late, enough time for them to get on and they arrive early. A tree had fallen a little closer to the rails than anyone would have liked but by the time it was noticed it was already gone.

They arrive, a car takes them to their second home and their partner embraces them as if for the last time. It will be the last time.

Twenty minutes later, exactly, as the partner serves them tea they fall over, tea spilling into the sheep skin.

They hold their partner, already dead, an aneurism, although they do not know this for sure, they mourn, grateful to have been there.

My work here is done.

***

It's snowing, I shiver but do not feel the cold. I mimic them on the bus, silently waiting, huddled together in the cold. Every once in a while someone curses the nails on the road, others remind them that what will be will be and I smile everytime. It is as if some of them had also seen the tree half a mile away falling under the weight of snow, the bus swerving off the cliff, no survivors.

Instead, they wait in the snow, an hour later the rescue crew finds them and they all return home.

***

She's late. She's early. A single gust of wind blows her hair in the wind and she shivers and that's all it takes for the other to see her and smile, promising internally she would never let her be cold again.

***

I place a hand on their shoulder, their chest heaving so slowly and yet so powerfully. I know nothing of death and what happens after, but I can ease anything for anyone, anywhere. As if they know I am here, the three family members in the room also place a hand on them and they glow, shining so bright as if the sun had shown through the clouds outside and will bring life into this room. It does, in a way, as they pass right through our fingers.

I stay with the family, as they sing and dance, as they move together. The body is washed not too far from here as I hold the storm for their body to be washed first. Other times I will beckon storms to wash bodies. They are buried, trees coming to life from their roots almost immediately.

They were one of the very few who had seen me.

***

I hear the calls of a baby in a womb. The midwife, one of the most skilled I've ever witnessed is saying things but the baby and I are in conversation.

They do not want to come out.

"And why is that?" I ask in my own way and they respond in theirs.

"I have heard of stories of this world and I do not want to participate," they say and I smile. This used to happen more often.

"And what is it you fear of this world?"

"What if I do not know to love like they do, what if their kindness is hard to reciprocate, what if in their generosity they devour every shield I have?" The baby calls back, pulling themselves farther into their womb.

"What if your love heals and guides them, what if your kindness becomes the bar of reciprocity, what if your generosity transcends time and space both?"

There's silence in the room, as if I had frozen time but I did not.

"And if I say no?"

"Then you have made your choice and it is yours and yours alone." I see time splitting, different timelines, both with and without them, every choice creating a new timeline, both with and without them.

I smile, and head to where I'm called next.

***

She doesn't like her neighbors. "I was here first" she tells me but I know she likes the company the younger cats bring her.

She walks off as soon as she sees them, the one with the beard and earrings, looking oddly similar to me. They scratch behind her ears and they walk together towards the sound of festivities in the distance. As they walk, a procession of cats follows them towards the naming ceremony.

Rana, she tells me her name is, as I walk along but she only ever looks at them and although they look at all the cats their eyes are warmest to her.

I see them in other lifetimes, she was their dad at one point, always never too far.

When we reach the party, filling the alleys with lights and the smell of jasmine filling the streets we both stand still at the entrance. The cats walk around, as if dancing to the music the humans dance to, taking water and food breaks from the foods laid out for them.

"Take care of them, will you?" She knows I will, I take care of them all, for I am the guardian of Falasteen, free always.

I don't respond, she doesn't wait for me to. She leaps and enters her next life with ease.

Overnight, their garden is filled with cactus and watermelon, both their favorites.

***

It is quiet, Jerusalem finally empty the hour after suhoor. The air is filled with intention, expanding the walls and reaching towards the sky, like Northern Lights in the center of the world. The love permeates, the warmth of bellies and children in bed, adults beginning to snore a lullaby in the final moments of a night sky that feels so light.

I wave my arms, conducting an orchestra of energy, revitalizing every soul, the ground shakes underneath cobblestones; mosques, churches, temples quiet a moment ago coming back to life, singing to the universe. Every soul lights up and the sun joins in, begging to be a part of the orchestra. They all do, Venus lighting up, the moon so close to being new and yet whole endlessly.

I do the same in every town, every city, they shine until the sun takes over and I move on.

Art by Nada

Diary of A Photographer

Noor Aldayeh (They/She)

Crowded town square
Amos laugh loudly
in tiny plastic chairs
Palestinian flags posted
every few steps

Two wrinkled hands
Atop a bedazzled,
Rainbow Quran
Jewelry glistens
Along the walls of the
Ancient, restored Souk

The elder,
Known for their bright smile
Lazes atop the shelves of
Their overflowing library

A boy
Riding a bicycle
Pedals into the driveway of
His great-great-great grandmother

Calligraphy pens

Soaked in

Rich, colorful ink

Dancing on pages

Of silk, papyrus

Everything handmade

Impossible not to spot

The art,

Nestled in every corner

Reaching out to be

Seen

The Sea of Galilee,

Mediterranean,

Dead & Red

Glisten atop smooth rocks

Three elders,

Sit between sand and water,

A tray of tea & salted nuts

Resting between them

A shutter flash then,
Splash

An animal sanctuary,
An orange tree, in bloom
Stray cats eating food
which has been left out for them

Concert scenes,
In ancient venues
Tattooed hands flying
Beside leather niqabs

The laughs of the
Kids in every neighborhood
Echo, reverberate, and
Enlighten the passersby

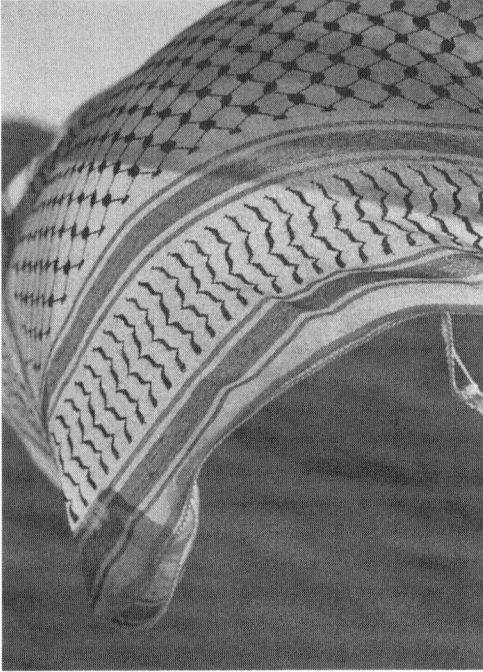

The best hummus and

The best Kunafa and the

Best Zaytoun and

The Best

Everything!

Poetry nights at

24-hour Coffee Spots

Sipping never-ending

Karak on tap

The Jiddo still works
At the Family bakery
And scolds the children
He sneaks Ma'amool

Yasmine and

Roses and

Apples and

Poppies and

More to stop and pick

Dinner shared on the floor

With gritty blur and
Arms that cross into interconnected
Webs

Teta's couch featuring
Ancestral embroidery and
A butter cookie tin
Full of sewing materials

A shared nightstand;
Home,
Land,

Signs and

Wildlife and
Sanctuaries

Kites flying outside
Car windows,
Young folks in colorful
Thobes and abayas and clothes

Parkour parks and
Theaters, a short walk then
Fresh juice from the corner stand

Birds and
Horses and
Doves

A distant relative's cookbook
Next to her great aunt's fishhook

This leather notebook
Bound by lover's hands
Awaits its next journey

Shot on film & digital
Next edition,
TBA

ليافا

خلقت بلا ظلم

وما الغصة
و حبيبي بين ثكنات الياسمين
يرتوي الشعر من انبياء عائلتي
يبوح العشق و العزة

و ما الذلة
وكياني يرقى
بين معاجم الفقهاء يروى
و في خيال الشباب يشتهى

و ما الفرقة
ورقصي يعترض المآرة
في أساطير الفن يحكي
يترنح بين لسان الشعراء

وما الجنة
و اليوم يقبّل الليل في جرءة
والحب يعلوا صوت جسدي
حين يهمس حبيب العمر ابقى

وما الموت

إذا شئت قدري

و دفنت بجوار أحبائي

خلدت

To Yaffa

Mama Ganuush (They/Them)

I was born without injustice

What is anguish?
While my beloved is amidst jasmine's serenity
Drinking poetry from the prophets of my kin,
Revealing love and honor.

What is humiliation?
My essence ascends,
Echoed among scholars' lexicons,
Desired in the fantasies of youth.

What is separation?
My dance confronts fate,
Narrating in the legends of art,
Swaying amidst poets' tongues.

What is paradise?
And the day kisses the night boldly,
Love's voice rises within my being,
When my beloved whispers, "Stay."

What is death?

If my time arrived,

And I'm buried beside my loved ones,

Immortal.

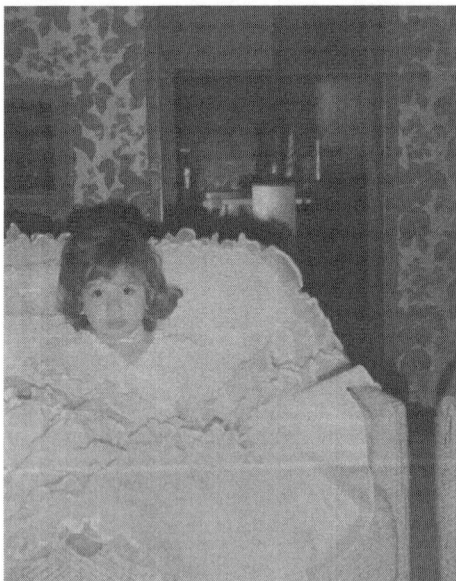

Contributors

رند

(she/her) @officialjakegyllenhalal

AB Bedran

(they/she) is a Queer Mixed Palestinian American based in Nashville, TN. Their relationship to poetry and art has been lifelong. They started writing about their experiences as a Palestinian in diaspora in adolescence and has expanded on this theme in their art as well.

Ali Khader

(he/him) I am here, I am there. Born in Kuwait, blood brought over from Anzah, my spirit in the sky and my body now nestled between grape leaves and olive trees. I love and I am loved. Hamdilla.

Aram Ronaldo

(he/they) is a queer/nonbinary/Palestinian/Armenian/Califor nian artivist and zine-maker-and-enthusiast living and working between New York and California. Aram makes zines which are often available at Bluestockings Bookstore in the Lower East Side of Manhattan and via their online store.

Car Nazzal
(they/she) is a writer, artist and sculptor. Nazzal's foundations for creating are based in psychology with practices uncovering the shadow through sensuality, mischief, and the creative process. Informed by their personal experience being queer, neurodiverse, and mixed-race to tell stories that are often silenced or taboo.

Duha Dahnoun
(she/her) is a young Palestinian writer and activist who enjoys the freedom of artistic expression and chooses poetry as a form of activism. She enjoys reading books by and about people who share her identity and loves the color of a Palestinian Poppy.

Haneen

(he/him) is a neurodivergent, queer, and trans Palestinian from Al-Quds (Jerusalem) & Nablus raised in Diaspora. He aims to embody the Palestinian spirit in every aspect of his life, from his activism to his hobbies and everything in between.

Jenan

(she/her) is a writer, researcher, and craft-maker from occupied Palestine. Jenan is interested in pedagogies of care, world-making, unsettling nature, and disability politics, among other topics. Jenan believes in a Free Palestine, by any means necessary.

Lama

(they/them) I am a Palestinian Egyptian settler in Toronto, born and raised in Cairo. A writer, educator and student of the Nile and the Mediterranean Sea. The sea and Nile are my ancestors, teachers, life-giving beings and the connectors that mould my imagination of liberation. Water does not obey borders, it is the physical manifestation of liberation for me. Like water, my writing does not submit to the system; it is my lifeline for truth-telling and actualizing liberation.

Mama Ganuush

(They/Them) a disowned, liberated, disabled, Palestinian, and Trans drag artist and social justice activist. The founder of House Ganuush, and Heritage Activists & Liberation Artists (HALA) collective.

Maria Zreiq

(she/they) Palestinian interdisciplinary artist and community organizer. Working predominantly with text and image-making through various forms including photography, documentary filmmaking, and poetry, her work examines notions of memory, longing, and resistance during times of political and social upheaval. As an organizer, Maria's practice centers on revolutionary pedagogy, culture production, and queer imaginaries.

Mays Salamah

(she/her) Mays is a Palestinian born in Jordan and currently residing on unceded Duwamish and Coast Salish land (Seattle). Mays is an editor, performer, tatreez artist, and writer. mayssalamah.com

Mishandi J. Sarhan

(she/her) I'm a Palestinian-American artist from SLC UT. I use my art to reconnect with my culture, to showcase our joy, resilience, and resistance, along with exploring ideas of our hope for the future and a Free Falastin.

Nada

(she/her) is an aspiring Palestinian actress. She dreams of one day gracing the theaters of Yaffa with her talent in a freed Palestine. She seeks to illuminate the stage with stories that resonate with her community.

Noor Aldayeh

(they/she) Noor Aldayeh is a queer Jordanian-Palestinian and Syrian artist creating media that dispels Orientalist depictions of the

SWANA world. Follow @nooraldayeh to keep up with their ongoing work!

noor il alb

(they/them) i am a multidisciplinary artist from bilad il sham. my work is informed by my love for nature, my homelands and the earth. my art is a prayer for the new earth, a future where we are all free. stay in the loop by signing up for my mailing list here:
http://eepurl.com/iMUjhM

Sonia Sulaiman

(she/her) Sonia Sulaiman writes speculative fiction inspired by Palestinian folklore. Her work has appeared in Arab Lit Quarterly, Beladi, FANTASY, FIYAH among other venues. Her stories have been nominated for a Pushcart, Lammy, and Best New Weird awards. In her spare time, she curates the Read Palestinian Spec Fic Reading list.

Summar

(She/Her) is a queer Palestinian and Lebanese interdisciplinary artisan who explores the relationship between objects, people, and space. Her work celebrates Levantine culture, and she often utilizes cultural motifs and signifiers in her art.

Yaffa

(She/Her) is an acclaimed disabled, autistic, trans, queer, Muslim, and indigenous Palestinian. They are the executive Director of the Muslim Alliance for Sexual and Gender Diversity (MASGD) & author of Blood Orange. In a Free Falasteen, Yaffa is a death worker and spirit healer.

Acknowledgments

At a time when so much is demanded of queer and trans Palestinians, I am grateful for everyone who responded to this call to envision a free Falasteen, whether they are included in this collection or not. Immense gratitude goes to friends and family who have supported my work over the years, directly or indirectly. Thank you to Andrea Ramos, who has supported this process in its entirety. Thank you to Mays Salamah, whose thoughtful edits for the pieces in this collection have served as a pathway to experiencing what art can be in a utopia. Thank you to Hannah Moushabeck and Michael Colgan for their care and thoughtfulness in reviewing this work. Enormous thanks to Eman Abdelhadi, for the brilliant introduction and for envisioning a free Falasteen years ago in their remarkable book, Everything for Everyone.

Finally, immense gratitude to all the visionaries who have been dreaming up utopias for millennia, especially the indigenous, Black, queer, disabled, and trans folks who have always seen beyond the fabric of possibility and expand it with every breath.

About Meraj Publishing

Meraj Publishing is a Trans and Queer Muslim publishing house that centers TQM voices from the global majority. Recognizing the vast inequities in the publishing industry, we aim to enable TQM individuals from the global majority to fully own our stories. Meraj prioritizes stories that focus on building utopia, hope, love, spirituality, and belonging. Meraj Publishing is entirely run and operated by the TQM global majority.

Other titles by Meraj Publishing:

Blood Orange by Yaffas AS